The Blue Wallpaper

Cover designed by Millie Carpenter and
Maxfield Lydum

ISBN: 9798657080100

For my parents, who taught me to reach for the birdies.

Was it a vision, or a waking dream?
Fled is that music:—Do I wake or
sleep?

John Keats, *Ode to a Nightingale*

Acknowledgments

I owe a debt of gratitude to so many people for their help and support in making this project happen.

Tucker, Kyle, and Santiago for their enduring friendship, guidance, and disc golf wisdom.

Ezra, Jacob, and Mick for their insight into so many things and for too many conversations to count.

Austin and Jared for their friendship, energy, and interest in making things fly far.

Erik, Jill S., and Robert for their leadership and creativity in making track and field happen.

The many great teachers I've had, including Joe, Ben, Rachel, Li, Tres, and Gantt for their kindness and their care.

Xander, Joey, and their families for their light and smiles.

Sam for their world-shaking power and facility with language, their thoughts, and their unceasing friendship.

My entire family, including Fred, Delores, Kathy, Debbie, Vicki, Jill, Glenn, Hazel, T, Jerri, David, Len, Chuck, and

Phyllis for shaping my world in beautiful ways.

Gary and Jill for their hospitality, humor, and generosity.

My parents Matt and Randi for boundless love.

Hazel for her sharp intelligence, her empathy, and her love for people.

Millie for checking in on me, for snacks, for hugs, for restful sleep, and for calm mornings.

Tuesday October 12th

she seems quiet even for her
She takes the stone stairs two at a time and pulls open the big wooden door of Anthony Hall. They walk down the hallway, their boots ringing against the dusty tile and the old wooden ceilings.

Everyone glances up when they walk through the door. Jess moves deliberately, holding her head high and striking her boots against the ground. Mandy follows behind her, keeping her eyes down. The instructor, Mark Whiteside, leans over his computer.

can't figure out his slides again
They take their seats in the middle of the lecture hall. It's 9:01 and he's stammering out an apology about his computer.

Randell lays in bed, wondering what Nigel's doing in the living room. A car rumbles over the potholes in the alley. Nigel knocks over what sounds like a box full of silverware.

In Anthony Hall, the instructor tries to move on with the lecture without the slides. The class is on histories of political violence. He chugs water from a plastic bottle and looks up at the clock. "I'm really sorry about starting late. We... We're going to continue our.... I wanted to start today by showing a video, but I'm terrible at technology and can't get my computer to work right now. So, we're going to continue our conversation about both the civil rights movement and more modern activism..."

Randell opens one red eye and stares at the ceiling. Nigel's singing a song in the living room.

The instructor pauses and waits for someone to answer. Jess looks up from her notes.

"Does anyone have an idea? If you've done the reading you might have some idea. How did MLK's religious background inform and shape his political strategy?"

Mandy keeps her head down, making quick scribbles.

The instructor tries to twist his head out of his tight collar.

Lapis enters campus through a hidden path in the hedges. The last of the morning mist is burning off, rising over the buildings and leaving the sky wide open.

"Do we have any ideas about that? Can we draw anything from our reading which might suggest a continuity between his religious ideals and his approach to civil rights activism?"

Lapis finds a wooden bench hidden under a Silk tree, a shady place where the mist's still rising and twisting through the hedges. She's skipping class.

Jess stares him down from her seat, not blinking. He meets her stare and panics, looks away and tries to regain his composure.

"How might we... What can we..."?

He's reaching for something intangible, some set of words which will bring forth the message. Something clear and sensible and honest. But he can't find words. He feels the fabric of his shirt sticking to his back. He turns and walks back to the lectern to grab the plastic bottle. And Jess follows him with her eyes. She watches with an even, neutral gaze. She's not waiting or expecting anything, she watches the sweat gather on his forehead.

Lapis watches bands of light beginning to spill through the branches above her. The light spills and spreads across the shady garden. She takes a long breath.

Mandy traces the outline of the small rabbit she drew, follows the outline faintly. He tries again to get the lecture going.

"I think what we have here is a series of examples which illustrate a long... uh, tradition. A long tradition or continuity between styles of political activity."

11

The light settles on the long grass in the garden, coming to rest softly. Lapis lets her breath rise slowly. The light twists gently through her hair. And she lets the breath fall smoothly, sinking deeper.

"So, what can we glean about MLK's political strategy if we understand it as arising from his religious background?"

His voice doesn't ring across the lecture hall the way other voices do. His question floats weakly away from him and wavers for a moment like a soft knuckleball before landing in the front row.

Mandy traces the rabbit closely, begins shading its ear faintly.

Jess watches him fidget, sees the desperation puddle up on his forehead. She glances up at the ceiling for a moment then turns her eyes squarely back on him.

"I have a problem with the premise of that question," she says calmly.

Several students turn their heads to face Jess.

"That's great Jessica! I…"

"Jess"

"That'srightI'msorry Jess! That's exactly the spirit of critical exchange we're trying to foster here."

"I have a problem," she continues when he stops to take a drink from the plastic bottle, "with this over-played notion of historical continuity. But I have a bigger problem with the way you're attempting to whitewash the activism of marginalized people."

She bears down on these last words and pauses for a moment.

"I don't think we're trying to conflate…"

"But the premise of your question is that Dr. King wanted everyone to just get along, to just forget about our country's racist history and move on. And that's just not true. He

12

wanted justice. And he was ready to use all kinds of methods, peaceful or not, to achieve that end."

The fluidity and patience of her speech make Whiteside's appear even more strained and desperate.

"It's not to say... I don't mean to imply...."

Mandy sketches inside the rabbit's other ear.

"And that premise ultimately erases the desperate measures marginalized people were forced to take in their activism. You're talking about the civil rights movement as a series of meetings where white people sat a table and gave marginalized folks their rights. And that's such a damaging and inept historical analysis."

She shapes the words gently with her hands, moving in relaxed flourishes, she gains even more confidence as she speaks, full-voiced, her words ringing in the lecture hall.

"I think the answer you're looking for is about white-washing Dr. King's legacy. Sure, his Christianity was a big part of his identity. But he was a radical, he knew people's lives were on the table, and he was willing to risk his life over and over again to find justice."

"B-"

"The voting rights act, which is now falling apart before our very eyes, was the product of people breaking laws. It was the product of people directly confronting their oppressors."

"How abou-"

"But you don't see it this way because you've never had to fight for the right to exist. It's dangerous, difficult, and exhausting work, having to claim space for yourself constantly."

The morning light's beginning to pour through the windows in the back of the lecture hall. Mandy feels the light covering her neck in warmth. She closes her eyes and draws a long inhale.

The lecture halls windows are designed to illuminate the front of the room where the instructor stands, but the old hall is

13

so poorly ventilated that the sunrise, which comes late and ripens slowly in October, begins to bake everyone inside the room. Whiteside feels his shirt tightening around him, cutting into his neck and sticking with sweat to every inch of his back. He tries again to take control of the conversation.

"I think we need to consider that this is a classroom. I'm trying to teach this class. And if you have these problems with... concerns about... my... approach, then perhaps after class would be a more... um...appropriate time to air those concerns."

"Your narrative," she cuts in effortlessly, "is about turning the struggle of marginalized people into some lesson about the value of playing by the rules. It's about erasing what makes you uncomfortable. Erasing the fact that it took violence for folks to earn a sliver of the freedoms that you've enjoyed since birth."

Whiteside lifts both hands and takes a step back.

"I'm sorry, but if you're going to continue in this way, I'll have to ask you to leave."

Mandy squeezes her eyes shut.

"Why is that?"

"I...it seems you have no interest in contributing to a productive discussion. You only want... you're just disrupting our class and making it impossible for everyone else to receive their education."

"You don't want to do this." Her tone does not change, she holds her gaze on him and won't let go.

"How about instead of kicking me out of your class you just engage with the questions I'm raising."

"You're not... I don't hear you raising questions, I hear you trying to start an argument. And that's why I'm asking you to leave now."

"I didn't mean to upset you, but I think what you're doing proves the necessity of my questions. Why is your first response to push back when I try to bring up what you're erasing?"

"Because it's beyond the scope of our discussion!" he raises his voice for the first time, but his anger doesn't make him appear more powerful, or give him an air of control. His anger emphasizes his weakness, his hurt. He's angry because she has the ability to tip his balance.

The light spills over the wooden seats row by row, warming Mandy's back. She draws another breath.

Lapis exhales gently, letting her breath fall slowly. The sparrows wait in the branches in the spiraling light.

"You are permitted to disagree, but you can't disrupt the whole class for your social justice routine," Whiteside pants, out of breath. He steps back again to lean against the podium.

"You're not going to like what happens next," Jess says as she closes her notebook.

"Please leave now," he begs, leaning his wet shirt against the podium.

Jess turns and places the back of a finger on Mandy's arm and rubs gently.

Jess mouths the words *I'm sorry* as she rises from her chair.

Mandy feels her cheeks beginning to burn.

"We have to go now," Jess whispers aloud.

Mandy quietly gathers her things, follows closely behind Jess down the stairs, and feels her cheeks burning as they cross the front of the lecture hall and out the doors.

Lapis rises from her bench and turns to the sparrows in the tree, watches them shift among the leaves. She runs the back of her hand up the tree's mossy side, lingering for a moment in the garden, before stepping out from behind the bushes and joining the clamor of noontime pedestrian traffic.

"Jesus fuck man," Randell grumbles as he staggers to the bathroom. "What have you been doing all morning to make so much fucking noise? And… for Christ's sake put clothes on."

He stumbles into the bathroom and turns on cold water.

Nigel's sprawled out on the living room floor with a bath towel wrapped around his waist.

"I've been reading," he calls from his spot on the floor. But the apartment isn't big enough to raise one's voice from anywhere.

Randell lets the water run down his face.

"I'm not much of a reader, but I never thought it was a very loud activity."

Nigel scribbles something in the margin of his book. Randell steps out of the bathroom. A few drops of water run down his chest. Nigel's note runs down the side of the page and begins to wrap around the bottom.

"Nigel," Randell says directly, "I'm talking to you. What was all the noise? It sounded like you dropped a bunch of silverware."

"Oh, that was when I was doing dishes." Nigel grins into his book. The note runs up-side down on the bottom of the page.

Jesus man," Randell shakes his head and walks through the short hallway and into the kitchen.

"Hey what the fuck happened in here?"

"What do you mean?"

"You moved everything around and put up wallpaper."

"I followed my impulse to do some organizing."

"Where's all the silverware?"

"On top of the fridge."

Randell walks back to the living room and stands above Nigel. The note wraps around the bottom of the page and begins ascending the other margin.

"But what did you organize?"

"Well I put things into places that felt were right for them."

"That's why the silverware's on the fridge?"

"That's why the silverware's on the fridge."

The note's making gradual progress up the margin, climbing over the lines of text one by one. Nigel's gaining steam, scribbling faster and faster.

"What are you reading?"

"Keats."

""Huh." He wonders for a moment if he's heard of that book before. "Jesus I think I'm still drunk. Don't you have class or something?"

"I do. In three minutes."

"It starts in three minutes?"

"It starts in three minutes."

The note's climbing higher, rounding over the edge of text, reaching for the top of the page.

"You'll be late then," Randell says as he plops onto the couch and rubs his palms into his forehead.

"I understand why you would think that," Nigel replies, "but I think I'll make it."

Randell rubs his forehead slowly. Suddenly Nigel jumps to his feet.

"That's all it is!" he shouts. His towel slips from his waist and falls to the floor.

"Why were you wearing a towel over your shorts?" Randell asks.

"It's about revealing," Nigel says, beaming.

"What?"

"Wow that's all it is. Revealing, disclosing, the ecstatic experience!"

"What are you talking about?"

"I have to go. Here's what I'll tell you. Revelation is a fragile, unstable, explosive mode. Separate from confessional I think."

"Sure it is man. You better go to your class." Randell kneads his palms into his forehead, "Jesus my head's killing me."

"I'll be back later tonight, going to the library for a few hours after my class."

"Don't have too much fun, shit."

Nigel flies down the stairs two at a time and bursts out into the bright October sun.

Randell reaches for the remote on the floor and feels the surge of hot pain light up his back.

"Fucking shit," he winces and drops to his knees.

"Damn it," he says through gritted teeth. After a few moments he tries to stand, but his back tightens again and he drops to the ground.

"Fucking shit" he grumbles as he rolls onto his back. The painful heat's pulsing down his lower back. He tries to press his feet against a wall to relieve the pressure. His back spasms each time he tries to get in position.

"That fucking... damn it"

Pressing his feet into the wall relieves some of the pain. He lays on the floor with his arms spread wide.

Just because she didn't know how to drive he thinks to himself.

Driven on that road a million times, knew it like the back of her hand shit drove it two three times a day sometimes

He presses his feet firmly against the wall, trying to relax the muscles in his lower back.

not paying attention just angry at me won't talk then BAM Jesus lucky no one was hurt

He tries to relax deeper into the stretch, feels another flash of heat surge up his back.

18

Except for me I guess

Randell squeezes his eyes shut.

Dumb thing, real shitty thing to get hurt doing nothing just sitting there. After everything I've done All that work carrying shit on my back

He takes shallow breaths, short and choppy.

Climbing trees in the dark running wild through the forest

He tries to imagine standing up without pain.

Like when those guys chased me deep up the mountain after it happened

He tries to slow down his breathing.

Up those logging roads all the way. Deep up the mountain

He tries a deep breath, drawing it slowly, expanding.

Those kids thought I had her with me idiots...big fuss for what....

But once his diaphragm expands it pushes up against the bad rib.

"Jesus! Damn it," he whimpers.

Big showdown on the mountain.... Waving their guns around like idiots for what

He moves slowly, trying to turn onto his stomach.

Cornered deep up on the mountain in the dark rain you done it now randell you done it now you had no right to hurt him you done it now

He needs to get ice for his back. Twenty minutes of ice and he'll at least be able to walk a little. He tries to push himself up to his hands and knees.

You're a damn foot Randell think you're above everybody so high and mighty well we'll see

He makes it to his hands and knees. Now if he can get to his feet, he can maybe lean against the wall down to the kitchen and grab a bag of frozen peas.

19

And those boys all hot and angry and scared

He takes a wavering breath and tries to rise up to his feet.

"Fuck!" he yells and drops back to his knees.

"Well this is great," he says after a moment.

Plenty of things to be scared of in those woods deep up the mountain.... scared to die out there alone in the rain. wolves coming back these days. hard to get up those logging roads. it would take days to find you up there

He crawls across the floor slowly.

But those boys weren't afraid of any of that

He crawls slowly, intentionally. His cheeks grow red from the effort.

No those boys were afraid of what they couldn't touch, could never understand

He reaches the fridge and pulls himself up as the pain shoots wildly across his back, pulls the bag of mixed vegetables from the freezer, spilling popsicles and a frozen pizza, before crumbling to the floor.

Shook them down to the core, like watching a face appear behind you in the mirror at night, a white face... that i would sacrifice everything. that i would go so far

He squeezes the bag under his lower back and settles down on the kitchen floor, breathing softly.

weird wallpaper Nigel pasted up there

And the frozen vegetables numb his back slowly.

Nigel walks quickly through campus, buzzing with the implications of his idea. He repeats the words again and again in his mind *fragile, unstable, explosive* as he passes under the massive English Oaks lining the walkway. He tries to bring forth the words with his fingers, rubbing them together slowly, churning the words over in his mind. *Revelation in moments of unstable ecstatic experience*

He tries to let the words pass through him as he walks, roll through his legs, hum in his shoulders. As he passes under the oaks, he tries to let the words beat through his chest and vibrate rhythmically through his body.

He's very late to class.

Across campus Mandy writes notes on the highest floor of Townsend Hall. Professor Lydia Mitchell speaks intentionally through her glasses, reading aloud from a massive text bristling with yellow page markers. She reads the poem slowly, her voice balancing for an instant on each word and bouncing on to the next one.

Mitchell looks up from over her glasses and scans the room.

"Can someone who is of age and enjoys the occasional draught of vintage please tell me what in particular appeals to you about wine?"

Twenty feet below them Lapis mounts the old spiraling staircase leading to the highest floor. She pauses at each window on her way up to examine the landscape below her. She pays special attention to the way her relationship to the giant Douglas Firs outside changes as she reaches each new floor.

"What does wine taste like?" she asks placing her tome on the wooden lectern.

"It's bitter," offers a student in the front row, "I actually don't like it."

"You don't like it, that's great!" says Mitchell with a smile.

Nigel becomes lost among the Douglas Firs outside Townsend Hall.

"It doesn't taste like a soft drink, it's not exactly sweet. So why the fuss?"

Mandy watches Professor Mitchell's eyes twinkle as she scans the room. She smiles to herself and begins shaping an outline of a small bird, content to sit and listen to the discussion unfold around her.

Mitchell turns her eyes to the back of the classroom. She smiles and nods as Lapis enters the room silently, without raising anyone's attention, and takes a seat near the door. She removes a small black book from her bag and places it on her desk.

"I'm interested," Mitchell continues, "in the kind of sensory experience Keats is setting up here."

Nigel imagines Townsend rising sharply from the forest as he follows the walkway to the front steps. Dusty light streams through the trees. The walkway is blanketed by brown needles.

"What this speaker really yearns for, I argue, is an experience of withheld passion. An immersion in sensory passion which has been restricted for whatever reason."

Mandy's bird looks over into the upper margin. She allows Professor Mitchell's words to wash over her like a gentle stream, the afternoon breeze floats in through the open windows.

"But this withholding is also a necessary part of the process of wine making. It needs to age, it needs to be withheld, in a sense, to become what it is. And this speaker is aware of this, it seems to me, they are aware that withholding has made the wine more desirable."

Lapis listens intently. She has not opened her book. She watches Mitchell's patient smile appear as she pauses in between phrases, the way her eyes crease softly as she smiles.

Nigel raises his misty eyes to the towering building, frozen in wonder.

Lapis immerses herself completely in Professor Mitchell's lecture, hanging on every word while remaining comfortably reclined in her desk, stretching her legs out from under her. She inhabits the space around her fully, filling it with herself. She raises her hand.

Mandy shades the bird's wing faintly.

22

"I have something to add to that reading," Lapis begins.

Mandy stirs from her daydream when she hears the new voice from the back of the room, a voice she does not recognize.

"Let's hear it," Mitchell replies with a smile, "but can you remind me of your name first?"

"Lapis," she says.

Mandy feels something quiver in her stomach.

"I see this act of withholding appearing in other places in the poem and with different implications. In stanzas four and five we get this sense that the darkness of this garden heightens the other modes of sensory experience, that not being able to see the flowers intensifies the speaker's experience of the flowers. So, withholding the visual creates space for a more impactful Romantic experience."

Mandy doesn't turn to look at her, she keeps her eyes on her notebook and tries to calm the tingling in her stomach.

"That is a wonderful addition to this interpretation, Lapis! And you've directed us towards a section of the poem that I'd like to examine closer in our last few minutes here."

Nigel flies up the stairs two at a time. When he reaches the highest floor, he stops to look out at the world of drooping boughs and needles.

"I want to look closer at the stanza just prior to the one you mentioned, which I see as forming another element of this speaker's project."

Lapis leans in earnestly.

Mandy taps her pen silently against her arm for a moment, then stops suddenly. She becomes very aware of the existence of her hands.

"The speaker enters a different sphere of consciousness not because of Bacchus, but as a result of the subtle powers of poetry itself. Poetry is, in a sense, a vehicle to this transformative space."

Nigel steps into the restroom on the highest floor. He leans forward and stares at himself in the mirror, letting the words reverberate warmly in his mind *fragile, unstable, the ecstatic experience*

"And the speaker seeks, really yearns, to sustain this experience and allow the transformation to take place."

Mitchell pauses and glances at the clock when she hears the rustling papers in front of her.

"And unfortunately, we are out of time so we will jump in from here next time and maybe consider the way the other poems develop Keats' project. Thank you all for the delightful conversation today."

Mandy packs her things away deliberately, very aware of the way her hands look. A small crowd gathers around Professor Mitchell. She makes a quick scan of the room before she leaves but doesn't see anyone new. Some students linger in the room to talk about their workload or the brilliant October afternoon unfolding outside. Mandy leaves the room quickly and alone. The hallway becomes flooded by the students from other classes. Mandy joins the stream and files down the narrow staircase slowly. People enter the stream on each descending floor and the crowd bottlenecks in the foyer of the ground floor. She makes her way slowly to the door, surrounded by a group of loud men pushing their way through the traffic, laughing and shouting. One of them yells something incomprehensible as he cuts Mandy off and trips her into the wall. Her bag spills open when it falls to the floor. The men don't notice as they shove their way out into the sunlight. Mandy stuffs everything together as fast as possible, a flurry of embarrassment and anger flowing through her.

Why can't you just watch, just pay attention, just show a little self-awareness

The crowd has thinned out when Mandy rejoins it and steps out into the brightness. She walks down the stone stairs and onto the walkway.

Or just a little fucking consideration that other people exist

"Excuse me!"

Mandy stops with a jolt when she hears the voice. She turns and sees someone jogging towards her.

"Excuse me," she says again and smiles. "I was behind you and saw you picking up your things. You left this pen."

She holds it out towards her. Mandy panics, tries to find some words.

"Oh, thank you!" she manages to blurt out.

"You're in the Romantic poetry class, right?

"Yes I am." Mandy tries to hide the trembling. "Are you?"

"Yeah! Well today was my first day, I just signed up for it."

"Oh cool. Thank you again for grabbing my pen."

"Of course! My name's Lapis. Just by the way."

"I'm Mandy." She struggles to breathe.

"It's a pleasure to meet you, Mandy," Lapis says with a gentle smile.

There's just a slight pause before Lapis continues.

"What are you doing the rest of the day? Any more classes?"

"Well, um. I don't know. I have some reading to do."

"Hey, so do I. It's a beautiful day. I was thinking about doing my reading out on the lawn by the library. Would you like to join me there?"

"Um. I'm not sure if..."

"If you have other plans, don't worry. I'll be there for a few hours. But if you come, I'll have some iced tea for you."

"Okay, I think I can make it."

"Wonderful. I hope I see you."

Mandy tries to think of something else to say.

"Okay," she says.

Lapis smiles and walks back to the bike rack. Her bike is alone on the rack, a black single speed with white tires.

Mandy walks under the Douglas Firs, replaying the conversation in her head, butterflies dancing in her stomach.

Lapis pedals through campus, gliding through the crowds.

In Townsend Hall, Nigel emerges from the restroom. He approaches the classroom slowly, remembering the way the words feel in his mind. He enters the empty room and stops, *ecstatic, revelation, fragile*

As the afternoon wears on, the sun begins baking the muggy upper wing of Johnson Hall. The old building is perfectly equipped to trap warm air and hold it there, stagnant. Several students sit on the floor of the hallway on the top floor, awaiting their appointments with the sociology advisor. The students shuffle their limp papers and look at their phones. In the office, Julie Andersen stares intently at her computer screen.

"So, you'll still need to squeeze in 12 more upper division credits to receive the minor. And hmm... those need to be passed with a grade of C or better."

The glare of the computer begins hurting her eyes in the afternoons when students come for their advising appointments.

"At least one of those courses needs to fulfill the research methodology requirement. I'd recommend the class on social inequities."

The students in the hallway stare at their phones and try to ignore the hot moisture in the air. The sound of heavy footsteps rings up the staircase at the end of the hallway and around the corner. Each step booms through the building. As the sound approaches, the floor begins to rattle.

Jess emerges from around the corner and the sound grows bigger. She walks quickly down the hallway, each step decisive and powerful, parting the muggy fog. The students look up from their devices. She pauses for a moment when she reaches Professor Andersen's door. She inspects a few of the fliers posted on an announcement wall. Then she turns to face the students sitting on the floor. She kneels down to the floor.

"Would it be okay if I snuck in for a word with Professor Andersen? It won't take long."

Before they have a chance to answer, Jess notices a student leave the office.

"It won't take long," she says again, and steps into the office.

"Oh Jess, it's great to see you!" Andersen says with surprise.

"Great to see you too Julie," she replies as she settles into the chair in front of her desk. "How are things going up here?"

"Well, it's kind of the same thing as usual. Doing a lot of advising right now. We had to cut back a little this year so unfortunately it's all falling on me right now."

"But they have plenty of money for the new football stadium, don't they?"

"Oh, I know, it's unbelievable." Andersen turns her screen away and rubs her eyes.

"Well, I'm sorry to barge in unannounced like this, I just didn't want to clog your inbox with more emails."

"Don't worry about it, I love when you drop by. I feel like I'm spending all my time answering emails these days, I miss out on the real work."

"Right," Jess says sympathetically. "I imagine it's difficult finding time for your own research when you're forced to do so much office work."

"It's part of the job. But I haven't made much progress on my inequities in education book, which I was hoping to finish this winter."

"That's going to be a great book," Jess says reassuringly.

"But what's new with you? How are your classes this semester?"

"Well, this is kind of what I wanted to talk to you about. Things are going fine, but one of my sociology classes is causing me a little unwarranted stress."

"Why is that?"

"I guess you could say I've been disappointed in our instructor's lack of sensitivity to the issues of marginalized communities. It's a class on histories of political violence, and the approach our instructor is taking... at its best it passively erases the history of the activism of marginalized people. At its worst, he actively subverts it."

Professor Andersen takes on a somber air.

"I'm really sorry to hear this, Jess," she says after a pause.

"I can deal with different kinds of historical lenses, even different opinions. All our lives we've been forced to deal with that, right? Intellectual freedom, sure. But today I was actually kicked out of class because I mentioned my problems with his approach. Do I even have to point out the hypocrisy of that?"

"You were told to leave the class?"

"Literally kicked out of the class because I wouldn't yield my position about the importance of acknowledging the increased risk marginalized communities take in activist work.

Andersen looks at the floor and thinks carefully.

"Have you thought of filing a formal complaint?"

"That's why I wanted to speak with you. I wanted to know what options I have. I know some people would just tell me to make a note of it in my course evaluation at the end of the semester. But I don't know if I can stand his… pardon my language, his bullshit that long."

"I hear you, Jess. And I'm glad you chose to come to me."

"There's another thing I'd like to add, that I just have to bring into this."

"By all means."

"I don't mean to sound unkind, but he just doesn't seem qualified to teach at the college level. Or teach at all maybe. He gets so flustered, so defensive. It seemed like he felt personally attacked by my criticisms and he couldn't stand for it. He had no way to deal with feeling insecure other than getting angry and kicking me out of class."

Andersen takes another pause.

"I would suggest you file a formal complaint. I'd be more than willing to help. We can find a solution to this. I can't speak about a colleague in this capacity, but I would be happy to help you in any way I can. You're an outstanding thinker and we want to create the best situation possible for you here."

"Thank you, Julie. I've taken up too much time. You have other students waiting to speak with you."

"Why don't you come back tomorrow, and we can talk more about submitting a complaint. Better yet, how about we meet at Presto's. Does three work for you?"

"That works. I appreciate you so much, Julie."

"I appreciate you too, Jess. I hope you have a good afternoon; I'll see you tomorrow."

The next student ambles into the classroom as Jess moves briskly back down the hallway. She exits the old building to a refreshing blast of cool fresh air and the glow of the fading October afternoon. She checks her phone, surprised to find that Mandy hasn't texted her. She feels a knot of anger forming in her stomach as she walks through campus, walking faster and faster as the knot tightens.

29

Why hasn't she texted me? No check in? No hey I'm out of class how are you doing? She's been out of class for hours I don't even know where she is or what she's doing

She feels herself growing angry as she leaves campus. She pulls out her phone and calls Mandy, feeling the knot tighten with each ring. She throws the phone back in her bag when she hears the first words of the automated voicemail message and speeds up even more.

How can she do this to me

The sunlight's fading fast, long shadows emerge from the base of the trees, growing larger and spilling into one another.

"So, what made you decide to take the Romantic poetry class?"

The fading sunlight tumbles through Lapis' hair. She lays on her side, propping her head up with her hand. Mandy lays in the same position on the other side of the blanket. In between them rests the iced tea along with a reusable container full of sliced peaches.

"Well," Mandy responds, "It's a requirement for English majors. I know that's a boring answer, but it's the real reason. The romantics aren't my favorite."

"What is your favorite?"

"I really like H.D and Millay and Auden sometimes. I don't know I just get the sense… I know it's cliché, but it's hard for me to take the romantics seriously. Like they think they have some secret knowledge that lets them see the world differently and gives them all these insights. It just feels like they're caught up in that masculine impulse to believe their own ideas are so unique and special."

Mandy becomes aware of her words and stops talking. She looks up from her fingers. Lapis smiles and waits for Mandy to continue, alert and attentive. Mandy begins again, gingerly.

"I just feel like so much of what we study in the humanities is the rambling shower thoughts of old white guys. Another cliché I know, but really, these guys just sat around and wrote what came to them while women did their laundry."

She stops again. Lapis falls onto her back and laughs at the sky. She rolls back onto her side and props her head under her arm again.

"But I really love Professor Mitchell," Mandy continues. I love her enthusiasm and... she's just really great. The fact that she's spent her whole life learning about them means that maybe they did have something to say."

"I really like her too," Lapis replies. She pulls a peach slice from the container and holds in her hand.

"What about you?" Mandy asks. "Are you an English major?"

"I'm a music major actually. At the moment. I don't know how long I'll stay with it. I don't really know how long I'll be in college."

"Why is that?"

"I'm from a really small town," Lapis replies. "I was one of the only people from my graduating class to go to college. There's a stigma around it, like you're too good to stay there and get married and raise a family, go to church. They just don't understand why someone would want to go study poetry or anything like that."

"Do you want to go back?"

"Oh no way. But I don't really feel like college is right for me either. I love learning, but I don't want to look at everything so analytically. I'd like to just enjoy the experience, not dissect it."

"You had some really insightful analysis about the poem today."

"That's nice of you to say. I honestly don't know anything about it. I just signed up for the class to read poetry. There's just something about Keats... I can't explain it."

She looks at the peach slice in her hand.

"I love discovering new ways of imagining experience, new ways of seeing the world. That's what music does for me. And sometimes poetry does too. With Keats... it's like he's finding ways of expressing the exact experience I want my music to express."

"What experience is that?"

Lapis weighs the peach in her hand and glances up at the giant Oaks above them.

"Yearning," she says. "I guess that's also a cliché. But I want to bring out the most hidden secrets, the ones we don't tell anyone, that sit in our hearts for years while we try to forget about them. I want my music to make people feel those secrets welling up inside them dying to get out."

Mandy watches Lapis' eyes as she speaks, the light playing with her hair, the golden peach held up against the fading sun.

"I'd love to hear your music sometime," she says.

Lapis turns back towards her. They're silent for a moment, watching each other's eyes.

The sun sinks slowly through the trees.

"What about you?" Lapis breaks the silence after a while. "What drew you to study English?"

"Well... I wasn't quite sure what I wanted to do. I've always loved reading, so English made sense. But mainly I wanted... I don't know."

Lapis smiles and waits.

"I actually wasn't planning on going to college. But my girlfriend... Jess, she was already set on going here. I kind of followed her here. I know that doesn't sound great."

"Why do you worry about how it sounds?"

32

"I don't know. It's not that I didn't want to go to college. I just never would have gone here if not for Jess."

"What else do you enjoy about being here?"

Mandy thinks for a moment, self-conscious about her delayed response.

"Well… I don't really…"

"Not to put you on the spot," Lapis says gently.

"I love the sunrise," Mandy bursts out suddenly. "And the way it smells first thing in the morning. But I don't see them usually because I can't get out of bed."

"What is it about the sunrise? How does it make you feel?"

"I don't know it just… I feel like I have a chance to really do something. Like there's something out there I can't see or touch. I know that doesn't make any sense."

Mandy looks back at Lapis, glowing in the dim light.

"You can keep going if you want," Lapis says.

"It just… feels like a beginning. Like everything's possible again."

The darkness spreads across the lawn slowly, running over the buildings and trees, closing in. Mandy notices the darkness suddenly, starting from a dream violently. The darkness fills her stomach with quiet dread.

"I have to go," she says softly. "I wish I didn't have to."

"Is something wrong?"

"I just really have to go. I'm sorry. I really wish I didn't."

"Do you want me to walk you home?"

"I…"

Lapis' eyes shine softly in the dim light, clear and soft, like nothing in the world is dangerous, like nothing hurts.

"I would love that."

They fold the blanket together and walk quickly, passing under the stone entrance of the library. The walkway in front of the library is well-lit, illuminating the old brick and stone facade rising into the night. High above them, Nigel's immersed in the fluorescent light of the reading room. He sits at a table among stacks of books, humming the words silently, humming low in his chest *the nightingale, the ecstatic experience, revelation fleeting softly*

Randell wakes up on the kitchen floor, unsure of where he is. He looks around the small room, confused about the refrigerator looming over him and the curtains floating above his head. It's totally dark. He tries to stand up and finds his back is frozen numb. He gathers himself onto his hands and knees and uses the wall to rise to his feet. He wanders around the apartment, trying to remember where he is. The numbness in his back makes walking difficult. His legs are heavy. He stumbles into his bedroom and tries to lower himself to his mattress on the floor. The streetlight pours through the dirty window. He tries to imagine lowering himself onto the bed, what it would feel like to sink and bend comfortably and easily. He notices a small glint of golden light on his windowsill, illuminated by the streetlights. He squints to focus on the light. He drops hard onto his knees, leaning forward to see. He suddenly knows exactly what it is, a home-made necklace with a shiny piece of yellow glass shaped like a peach lit up by the streetlight.

"Fucking shit," he whispers, falling forward onto his stomach. Across town Mandy and Jess detour to the well-lit portion of campus, walking under the streetlamps. Lapis wheels her bike along.

In a small white house east of campus, nestled among the maple trees, Jess brings water to a boil. As the steam rises, she washes a lemon, places it on a cutting board, and splits it with a knife.

Lapis' bike clicks gently as she rolls it along.

"Thank you for walking with me," Mandy says.

34

"Of course, no need to thank me. Nobody should walk home alone. This place could really use some more lights."

Mandy watches the sidewalk unfold before her with each step.

"So, what do you imagine yourself doing after college?" Lapis asks.

"I'm not sure. Jess wants to go to law school. She could get in anywhere."

"So you want to wait and see where she's going and then think about it?"

"Well…"

I'm not sure it's what I want

"Wherever she decides to go will be an exciting place."

Ever since that night

"It's hard to say."

Ever since that night… I'm not so sure

"If it helps, I have no idea where I want to be. I just want to be somewhere."

She finally told me

"Yeah… "

She cried and cried and said it would never happen again, he was just some guy back in Portland it would never happen again

"Somewhere else with new people. That's my small-town angst talking I guess," Lapis says.

But I knew there were others… and she cried until I felt like it was my fault, like she needed more than I can ever be

"I'd love to meet Jess sometime. She seems like an amazing person."

And I knew I needed to get away, get so far away run into the mountains to the dark belly of the forest and bury my face in the needles…

Mandy and Lapis walk quickly down the dark tree-lined street towards the small white house on the corner. The front room is lit up brightly behind white curtains.

"Thank you again for walking with me. Are you sure you're all right by yourself?"

"I'll be great. It's a short ride from here."

They're silent for a moment.

"I know we didn't do much reading today. Maybe we can try again after the next class."

"Okay."

"Also, one more thing. I'm playing at a house show this weekend. You should come and bring Jess."

"Yeah that would be fun."

Mandy feels the trembling in her stomach again, nervous shaking.

and rise in the darkness and scream, cry, rinse myself in the frozen stream, forget everything

"Okay, get in out of the cold. I had a great time hanging out with you Mandy. I'll see you later."

Lapis pedals into the cold night, disappearing quickly down the street. Mandy stands outside the house, watching a shadow move behind the curtain. She walks towards the door. *and in the morning climb to the top of the mountain and watch the light peak over across the continent, watch the light opening the world, stretching out for me… and she'll be there eyes glowing in the sunrise, looking at me like she did in the grass*

Mandy enters the house. It's silent. Jess' mug is still steaming on the table in the living room.
And she'll never look away

She walks across the room, her steps drawing long whiny creaks from the wooden floors. She waits in the middle of the room, listening. The silence rings off the walls.

Lapis rolls her bike into her apartment and leans it against the wall. She sets her bag on the floor and takes out the container of sliced peaches. She takes a seat on the floor against the wall and eats the peaches slowly. She takes each bite deliberately. The apartment isn't entirely furnished yet.

Mandy watches the steam rising from Jess' mug. The table would normally be covered with several open books, stapled packets of paper with pink and yellow highlights running across them. But tonight, the mug sits by itself, a slice of lemon resting at the bottom.

Lapis chews the peach slowly with her eyes closed.

Mandy walks quietly across the living room, past the Audre Lorde poster hanging on the wall. She walks down the short hallway to their bedroom. The door is closed.

Lapis chews slowly, she leans her head back against the wall, presses her hands against her heart.

Mandy opens the door, trying not to make any noise. She enters the dark room and changes into her sleeping clothes. Not even Jess' breathing breaks the silence.

Tears hang delicately off Lapis' eyelashes. She draws a long inhale.

Mandy sinks onto the bed slowly, trying not to disturb Jess.

Lapis holds her breath inside of her comfortably.

Mandy settles onto the bed. She gradually becomes aware that Jess is not asleep.

Lapis reaches into her shirt and brings out her necklace, holding the small glass peach in her hand and rubbing it with her thumb.

Mandy closes her eyes.

Lapis rubs the peach gently, tears rolling down her cheeks.

"Where were you?" Jess asks simply.

"I was with a new friend I met in class." She tries to keep her voice from wavering.

"Why didn't you let me know?"

37

"I…"

"You didn't answer my calls or my texts because you were with a friend?"

"I'm sorry I…"

"Why couldn't you just update me?"

"I didn't think I needed to… update you on everything I do."

"You don't. But after that shit show in class this morning I just thought you would want to check on me, make sure I'm okay, stuff like that. After I got kicked out of class for standing up for what's right."

"I went with you… I didn't know you wanted to talk about it."

Jess doesn't say anything for a moment, disappearing into the dark room.

"Are you okay?" Mandy asks.

"So that friend is the person you were with when you got here," Jess says.

"Yes."

"What's their name?"

"Lapis."

"Lapis. And what were you talking about outside?"

"She invited us to a house show this weekend."

Jess doesn't respond.

"I'm sorry I didn't reach out and see how you were doing."

"It's okay I just had a hard day," Jess says as she rolls onto her shoulder, facing the wall.

Mandy stares at the ceiling.

"It wears me out," Jess says after a while. Mandy doesn't respond.

"I feel like I'm up against this whole university. And they say they're trying to foster debate and intellectual freedom and all that bullshit. And everybody just goes along when there's all this violence everywhere."

"But you're not alone," Mandy says.

Jess doesn't turn away from the wall.

"I know," she says quietly.

Lapis lays on the floor of her apartment, moving her lips silently. She mouths the words quickly and precisely, curling up on the floor. Apart from the bike leaning against the wall, the room is mostly empty. Two orange milk crates sit together in a corner. A guitar case rests on the crates.

Mandy stares at the ceiling. She listens to Jess' breath ease slowly as she falls asleep.

Lapis forms the words completely and silently. She sinks into the melody, giving each note its full length. Tears gather on the floor. When the song is over, she curls up tighter into herself. She presses the peach firmly between her palms as she falls asleep.

Mandy lies awake on her back, remembering in fleeting glimpses the way the fading light danced through Lapis' hair *and never look away from her*. She drifts to sleep as the birds begin to chirp, just before the first light peeks through the trees.

Wednesday October 13th

Nigel runs his hand over his new wallpaper, pleased with the way the morning light makes it look. He moves his hand quickly back and forth, then places his right hand next to his left, sliding them both quickly across the wall. He takes a step back and looks at it again. Because the kitchen is too narrow to get a look at it all at once he climbs onto the counter and squats low, inching up to the window to get the best look possible.

He's just returned from the library. He stares at the wallpaper for a long time, paying careful attention to how it makes him feel. He hears Randell emerge from his room, grumbling, and open the faucet in the sink. He closes his eyes. He begins paying careful attention to the way the wallpaper makes him feel when his eyes are closed. He hears Randell approaching, then hears him let out a loud sigh.

"Now what the hell are you doing?"

"I'm paying attention to how the wallpaper makes me feel."

"Oh, for Christ's sakes what the hell does that mean?"

"I'm seeing if I like it."

"Why don't you get off the counter, fucking hell."

He grumbles as he pulls a box of cereal from a counter. Nigel opens his eyes.

"I'm going to change it," he says finally.

"Change what?"

"The wallpaper."

"But you just… for fuck's sake you just put this one up!"

"It's not working quite right."

"What do you mean it's not working it just hangs up there!"

"It's not affecting me the way I thought it would."

"For fuck's sake…

How the fuck did I get stuck with this guy

"I thought it would make me want to crawl into the wall, mesh with it, that's what it needs to do."

"You gotta stop saying stuff like that."

"Like what?"

"Fuck's sake. What's a mesh?"

"Things overlapping so completely they become part of one another."

Randell fumes silently to himself for a moment.

"Okay you have to get off that counter now."

40

Nigel hops off the counter. Randell's surprised when he notices how much taller than Nigel he is.

Why haven't I noticed that before

He tries to calm himself down. He grabs the box of cereal and begins pouring some into a bowl.

How have I not noticed that? I could have sworn he was about my height

"You were pretty quiet last night. I didn't even hear you come in."

Nigel places his hands on the wall again.

When he came right up to me in the park

"I got here about 20 minutes ago."

Randell stops pouring and looks up in disbelief.

"You're shitting me, you just got here... you were there until 8 in the morning?"

"I was." He pushes his fingers against the wall, becoming absorbed.

"Doesn't that place close ever?"

"Midnight on the weekdays."

"So, what did you do all night?"

"Reading mostly, some writing."

"The whole night?"

"Well after midnight I had to leave the reading room and go somewhere in the stacks for a while."

"You hid?"

"Not for very long. I take my books with me and pretend to leave with everyone else. But I find a place in the deep stacks where security never goes. Security stops doing their rounds at one usually, so I go back to the reading room. Eric the custodian comes by around two and we talk for an hour. We have great conversations, you'd like him. Then it's pretty quiet for about four hours until it opens again at seven."

Randell stares at Nigel, a grin spreading across his face. Nigel steps away from the wallpaper and turns towards Randell.

41

"People start showing up around eight. Sometimes I stay until lunch, but I started thinking about my new wallpaper. I realized that since I installed it later in the morning yesterday, I hadn't seen it with the light from our window shining on it. From the east, from the sunrise. I got back here as fast as I could."

Randell turns towards the wallpaper and looks at it.

"And it wasn't what you wanted, huh? Well, you'll get 'em next time."

Randell takes his cereal and walks back to the living room and plops on the couch.

Weird guy, imagine what the guys back home would think of him, talking crazy like that

Nigel looks out the window, watches the sun cresting over the hills east of campus.

But it was real big of him to give me a place to stay here, gave me a month to find a job

He watches the sun clear the tree line and spread widely over the valley.

When everyone else was done with me

He rests his hands on the windowsill and draws a deep breath.

To take a chance on a guy living on the streets, under the bridge in the park, brought me in when everyone else was done with me

The light illuminates the dark silhouettes of the massive trees surrounding campus.

My parents, everyone back home, coach, the guys... Lapis... left me with nowhere to go...done

Nigel wants to be among the trees.

"I'm going back to campus," Nigel tells Randell as he enters the living room.

"Christ's sake man don't you ever sleep?"

Nigel's looks up at the ceiling.

"What are you doing on campus?"

42

"I have some classes later."

"Well, okay then."

Nigel moves towards the door.

"Hey Nigel."

"Yeah?"

"Take care of yourself out there."

Nigel smiles at him for a moment.

"I might bring back some new wallpaper with me," he says as he leaves.

A row of scarlet oaks line the street along the western entrance to the university. Together, the row of trees forms a wall of bright red leaves, a fiery barrier between the university and the city outside of it. The campus is quiet in the afternoon. When classes disperse the students file out onto the lawns and spread out over campus. There's a heavy sleepiness in the air. It's cool and cloudy.

Traffic stacks up quickly on the other side of the scarlet oak row. Students cross the street in large groups as the cars and trucks wait. By the afternoon, the exhaust from the vehicles grows into a large cloud hovering over the block.

The Presto cafe is a narrow brick building at the end of the street. Its big front windows face the long row of idling vehicles. But inside, the smell of chai lattes and fresh croissants offer an escape from the hazy clamor of the afternoon. Students are scattered around the room, books and computers on the small tables. Jess arrives at 2:30 and finds a two-person table near the front windows. She opens her computer and returns again to the university's political science website, where she navigates to the faculty page. She scrolls to the bottom of the page and clicks on Mark Whiteside's name, bringing up his academic profile. She spends a moment looking at his profile picture, notices the familiar gleam of sweat across his forehead and the stiff collared shirt squeezing on his neck.

and that asshole smile, like clearly, he's never been told to shut the fuck up

She opens his curriculum vitae again, scanning over it closely.

undergrad at his tiny little private school no one's ever heard of

She leans in closer to her screen.

that means two hundred thousand bucks of his investment banker dad's money to go to a shitty little private school and hang out with other mediocre white boys with rich parents

She scrolls through the document, looking for anything of significance.

Grad program at a football school...again, out of pocket...virtually no relevant publications during grad school...barely any conference presentations...no engagement with women scholars or scholars of color

She closes the laptop but keeps the tabs open. She takes out her notebook and looks over the ideas she outlined this morning. Underneath these notes, she adds her observations derived from his curriculum vitae. When she finishes writing, she closes the notebook and looks out the window at the line of traffic stacking up outside. She yawns and rubs her eyes. She checks her phone, finding no new messages.

damn it Mandy

She tries to think about something else. She looks out the window again, watches the cars roll slowly past her.

these walls block the sound from the street pretty well

Just before three, she walks to the counter and orders an iced coffee. Julie walks through the door just as she returns to her seat.

Across town Randell emerges from the apartment into the cool afternoon. He stands just outside the door and winces at the clouds.

Jess and Julie embrace in the cafe.

"Thank you for meeting me here."

"Any excuse to get out of that stuffy office."

Randell tries to take a big breath and starts coughing loudly.

"I was thinking about our conversation yesterday, and I wanted to make sure I wasn't putting you in an uncomfortable situation by speaking with you about one of your colleagues. I just needed to get those things off my chest."

"I want you to know you can always come to me and speak out about issues you're facing. It's our job, it should be our absolute top priority, to ensure that you feel safe. That you won't be forced to engage with needlessly traumatic material. I'm here to validate the way you handled that situation."

"I appreciate that so much. I was thinking about something else after our meeting yesterday. You were talking about the department's funding challenges. How you're having to take on such a heavy advising load and different things of that nature."

"Right, it's certainly not an ideal situation."

"Well, I was just wondering, and again, I mean no disrespect by this, but why hire this guy, Mark Whiteside, in the middle of these financial challenges. What exactly does he bring to the department that make hiring him necessary?"

Julie is silent for a moment; she thinks carefully about how to proceed.

"And I was just thinking," Jess continues, "apart from the issues I've been facing in the class, He just doesn't seem like a great candidate for a position in a department like ours. I thought we were trying to recruit more women, more people of color."

45

"I wasn't part of his hiring committee," Julie says quietly.

Jess feels her composure beginning to break slightly.

"And then I look on his CV and don't find any engagement with women scholars or scholars of color. His research, and here's the problem, seems to follow the same patterns of erasure that show up in his teaching."

"Jess, I hear you. You have the option to submit a complaint to the department. We have a committee dedicated to instructional quality and they'll give him the guidance he needs."

She feels herself growing angry.

"But that's not good enough. He's teaching classes at this university and actively erasing the issues of marginalized people. He's doing the opposite of what he should do. He's undoing the work that you and other great professors are doing. Can't we do more?"

"Let's submit the complaint and see where it goes. I'll advocate for you and make sure the committee hears the concerns you're raising."

"And what if they decide to do nothing?"

Julie doesn't respond right away.

"Julie, they hired this guy in the middle of a budget crisis. They fucked up. They must have thought he was something he's not. Maybe he's great at interviews, I don't know. But now he's standing in front of lecture sized classes teaching a whitewashed version of political history."

The desperation begins to grow in Jess' voice.

"Jess..."

"Meanwhile they looked you straight in the eyes and told you to sit in your office and help frat boys sign up for classes when you should be working on your book. You're the best writer in the whole department, doing the most important research maybe in the whole university, if they actually gave you the time to do it."

"Okay, I hear you…"

"And I'm telling you there's a man kicking students out of classes if they challenge his authority and the solution is complain to the people who hired him? He kicked me out of class. Is that an equitable outcome? Is there a theory of Marxist pedagogy that explains that?"

"I know you're upset, Jess. You have a right to be. I'm upset too. I want to fight them with you."

"Then fight them with me. Don't tell me you're on my side then tell me to fill out a form and wait four to six weeks."

"I'm on your side."

"Do you think he should have a job here?"

"I'm sorry, I can't…"

"Do you think he should have a job here?"

"Let's take a step back."

Jess buries her face in her hands. When she looks up, she drives her eyes hard into Julie.

"He's unqualified, never prepared, bullshits his lectures, and teaches a dangerous ethic of social respectability and playing by the rules. There's literally nothing redeemable about him as a researcher or teacher."

"I can promise you; he will hear these criticisms from people in the department."

she can't do anything, what do I want, for her to risk her job, hurt her reputation with her colleagues. that's not fair

"I'm sorry, I know your hands are tied."

"Filing the complaint will help, trust me. I know institutions are frustrating, infuriating even. But this will help."

Jess nods and looks out the window again. She's silent for a moment, staring through the line of traffic, to some place else on the other side.

"These walls block the sound from the street pretty well," she says.

Julie looks out the window and up the street, where the vehicles split off left and right under the fiery wall of scarlet oaks. The highest dark towers of the university rise from behind that wall of trees, looming over the mess of traffic and walkers below.

On the other side of the scarlet oaks, Mandy settles onto a bench and brings out her heavy collection of poems for the Romantic writers class. She returns to the John Keats section of the anthology, flipping through the poems, looking for the *Nightingale*. When she finds the page, she reads it again slowly, working to conjure each image completely in her mind. She looks up from the page and tries to remember Professor Mitchell's lecture. She sits up straight on the bench and watches the red leaves sway in the wind.

she was saying that wine is...that the reason we.... that wine gets better when it waits in the dark, when it's kept in the darkness for years, becoming itself silently

From her position on the bench, the row of scarlet oaks blocks the view of the street beyond it.

and this speaker wants to have the darkness, it's kept in the dark that's why she wants it it's hidden she said a draught of vintage... that she can't have it have and wants the hidden darkness

The breeze whirls through the red leaves, picking some up off the ground.

she says fly away to thee because she wants it and it's been holding her back wants it and if she can just have it

The breeze picks up, she sees it moving through the red leaves.

but it's not about having it... you can't have it... it's....music making secrets well up inside you that's what Lapis said music making secrets well up inside you dying to get out

48

She leans forward and watches the red wall of leaves vibrate in the wind.

that the secret will get so massive that it needs to come out, raging to the surface out of control

She looks back down at the page.

I cannot see what flowers are at my feet I cannot see what flowers are at my feet

She feels the wind blow against her face, through her hair.

and Lapis held the peach in her hand and ahh she looked at me and i've never ever seen eyes like hers

The wind picks up and blows leaves down the street.

and i promise nobody has ever ever looked at me like that...those eyes, I almost died

Students cover their heads and brace themselves against the wind as it whooshes down the street. Mandy sits still on the bench.

and when i heard Jess leave this morning, I closed my eyes and brought the memory up from inside me, brought her hips curving against the light pouring through the trees, brought the peach wet and glistening in her hand, strong shoulders in her tank top....and she pulled her flannel over them and walked me home and once her hand brushed against mine and I felt it first like a shock and I couldn't breathe then like warm rain

Mandy's eyes are frozen forward, transfixed on the space somewhere out in front of her.

I watched her lips move and my heart hurt, because what I want is the darkness and what she wants is bring it out

Her eyes grow watery as she stares forward. She doesn't notice Jess crossing the street, passing through the wall of red trees.

and i closed my eyes and imagined that when i opened them i would see her there beside me in the hidden darkness

49

"Thanks for waiting for me here," Jess says as she approaches.

Mandy stirs from her trance, alarmed.

"The meeting took a little longer than I thought it would."

Mandy tries to orient herself.

"I'm sorry about that," she says.

"It's windy out here."

"Yeah. I guess it is."

"Are you okay?"

"What? Oh, yeah, I'm okay. I was just reading."

"Come on, let's get home. That meeting was a shit show."

Jess takes Mandy's hand as she rises from the bench.

"I'm losing faith in this university's ability to do the right thing ever in any scenario," she begins.

"It's just so unbelievably frustrating and Julie... it's just getting too much. I thought at least Julie would listen and understand and know what to do."

Mandy watches the ground unfold below her. She doesn't say anything.

her hand running down my arm, falling into her...sinking...darkness

"And she has every reason to be infuriated that someone like him got hired in the middle of a budget crisis. He's not special, he's not a brilliant scholar or teacher, he's just a white dude who went to some good schools. And he sucks at his job. Like think about some of the other professors you've had here. You've had Julie before, you've had Ernst. How does this guy even belong in the same department as them?"

Mandy steps onto a red leaf. She doesn't say anything.

"How can she just…"

Jess takes a glance at Mandy.

"Are you listening? You're not listening."

50

Mandy starts from her thoughts.

"I'm sorry I… I was just caught up in my reading. I'm really sorry, no he's not anywhere near the teacher they are. I'm sorry."

"It's okay."

Jess keeps her eyes forward, she doesn't continue.

When they arrive at home, Mandy heads directly to the kitchen and sets her bag down on a chair. She fills a tea kettle with water and places it on a burner and begins boiling water. Jess sits down in her chair in the living room and arranges her study materials, drawing forth books, stapled packets of paper, pink highlighters, and her computer. Mandy watches the steam begin to wander out of the kettle in thin tendrils. She hears the familiar sound of keys tapping from the living room. Besides the faint noise of the wind outside, the keys tapping is the only sound in the house. The thin wavering band of steam grows steadily larger. Mandy watches it closely, filtering out of the kettle through the narrow spout, disbursing into the air, disappearing as it floats to the ceiling. Then she hears a voice from the living room. It's a familiar voice, one of their friends. She hears Jess laugh loudly. Soon the whistling of the kettle overwhelms the sound of Jess' conversation. Mandy pours water into the mug. She carries it carefully to Jess' table. Jess doesn't look up from her computer as Mandy sets it down on the table, gently resting it on a wooden coaster. Mandy walks to the window and watches the branches of the Douglas firs wave in the wind. Her eyes begin to wander down the street.

she held the peach in her hand and looked at me, asked me what I wanted to be… i still feel that in my stomach, that imprint of her eyes glowing in the fading light, like no one has ever looked at me before

She cranes her neck to see farther down the street.

where she rode off and disappeared under the streetlights

51

Somewhere behind her she hears the sound of Jess speaking, indistinct mumbling rising from far away.

Lapis takes care not to bump or scratch the walls of the stairwell with her bike as she carries it down the stairs. She carries the bike in one hand by its crossbar, holding the handlebars with her other hand to prevent the front tire from turning and hitting the walls of the stairwell. Once she clears the stairs and opens the front door to the blustery afternoon, she straddles the bike. She pauses for a moment to zip her denim jacket over her blue flannel shirt, before she pedals off smoothly down the street.

She rides quickly through the neighborhood adjacent to campus, gliding around the potholes and cracks in the road. She enters campus through a small hidden path behind the library. The path begins as a narrow slit in the hedges that line the street on the south edge of campus. It is an unmarked opening in the hedges which runs all the way through to the over side. She slips through the slit and rides carefully down the narrow path, climbing slowly over roots and rocks, bushes and shrubs growing on each side of her. When she emerges from the other side of the hedge, she hops off the bike and walks. The path widens into a trail of fine gravel, winding into a small green space with long grass, weeds, and indecipherable stone markers on the ground. The path disappears into the long grass. She walks slowly through the abandoned garden, listening to the wind whistle through the trees. The area is a mostly unmaintained section of campus, hidden behind the library, invisible from the street on the other side of the hedges. The thick shrubs surrounding the garden make the library's back brick wall mostly invisible. An old silk tree grows in the middle of the garden, its ranging branches spreading over the tall grass. Apart from the old, moss-covered stone markers and the back wall of the library barely visible through the shrubs, the only landmark is an old wooden bench, itself mostly covered in lichen and moss.

Lapis walks through the garden, listening. She stops under the silk tree and closes her eyes, paying attention to her breath. After a few moments, she continues to the other side, to where the fine gravel path reappears and leads through the trees, around the side of the library, joining the main walkway. She remounts the bicycle and pedals through campus, passing groups of students huddling against the wind. The walkway leading to Townsend hall climbs a slight incline, lined on both sides by the campus' oldest Douglas Firs. She takes special care as she navigates the narrow stairwell, carrying the bicycle. She reaches the second highest story of the building and rolls the bike along. Only a few professors remain in their offices, many of the doors are locked shut. Lapis wheels her bicycle through the hallway, resting it against the wall outside of Professor Mitchell's office. She steps into the doorway. Professor Mitchell's sitting in the dim office reading an old book, several lit candles rest on her desk. Lapis taps lightly on the opened door.

"Hey, professor, do you have a few moments?"

"Lapis! Yes of course come in and sit down. I was so glad to meet you yesterday and for you to join the class."

Lapis enters the office gingerly, trying to avoid stepping on a box of papers or stack of books.

"I'm really excited about it," she says as she sits down. "Wow, this office is amazing. I've never seen so many books packed into such a small space."

"Thank you, it's a pleasant little enclave here. I love opening the windows in the spring and letting in the smell from the cherry blossoms. You know, it's good that you're here right now because I actually had a question..."

Lapis leans forward slightly. Professor Mitchell moves several papers off her keyboard and looks at her computer screen for a moment.

"Well you still weren't showing up on my list after class yesterday. I thought it would probably get processed by today, but I just checked, and it looks like it still hasn't gone through."

"Oh, that's kind of odd."

"Don't worry about it, I'm sure something's going wrong on their end. I don't really know how the registrar operates. They're kind of a stiff bunch over there. I usually try to stay out of their way. Had some weird interactions with them back in the 90s, most of this was still on paper back then. But, in any case, I just wanted to make you aware of that."

"Thank you, that's related in a way to what I came to speak with you about. The bookstore was sold out of the Romantic poets anthology, so I'm having a little trouble keeping up with the reading."

"That's another bunch of stiffs, the bookstore people. I went on one date with the manager about 15 years ago, one of the most boring dates of my life."

"Oh, wow. He just wasn't interesting?"

"Not only that, he voted for Ross Perot! You might not be old enough to appreciate the significance of that, but things definitely weren't destined to work out there. You know, now that I think of it, that means the date must've been...20, 25 years ago. In any case, the bookstore."

"Right, the bookstore." Lapis smiles warmly at her from across the desk *what a beautiful soul*

"That date was 25 years ago and since then I've had so many problems with that place. Always seems to be some kind of hang-up with the books I order. He might be a little bit of an asshole. Anyway, the last few years I've been really looking for ways to use digital tools to enhance literary studies, so I've uploaded all the readings to the course site. Have you been able to access that?"

"No, I haven't yet."

"Oh, well of course not because the registrar hasn't processed your enrollment yet. Well, let's run down to the copy machine...actually, how about you just take this for a few days."

She rises from her desk and walks over to the wall of books on the other side of the office and plucks one from the top shelf without hesitation.

"It's an older edition, so you might have some issues with pagination, but all the poems are there. It should work until the registrar finishes with whatever they do over there."

Lapis holds the book with both hands.

"Wow, this is... thank you so much, you don't know how much I appreciate this."

"I'm happy to help you any way I can, there's probably lots of my handwritten notes in there, ignore those, they probably won't help you" she says with a smile.

"Professor..."

"You know, if it's comfortable for you, call me Lydia."

"I just really appreciate you letting me borrow this."

"I'm really glad you'll be part of our class this term."

Lapis watches the glimmer in her eyes when she smiles.

what a gorgeous person, amazing, beautiful light of a person

"Well, I guess that's all for right now. I'm sure you're ready to go home. But I'll definitely be back next week to share some ideas about these poems."

"Excellent! It gets lonely up here sometimes in the ivory tower, I love having students come by and sharing what they're working on. You know... I'm sorry, not to change the subject, but that's a really cool patch on your jacket. Is that who I think it is?"

Lapis looks down and pinches the denim between two fingers and brings it out closer for Professor Mitchell to see.

"This was the first patch I added to this jacket and she's still my favorite. Are you also a Joni fan?"

55

Professor Mitchell leans in to get a closer look at the patch.

"My relationship with Joni," she begins, "is cosmic to say least. And I think our last names are an interesting way of bringing that connection down to Earth in a sense. But I just love that patch, wrapped up in blue."

"I've been thinking about how Joni fits in with the Romantic writers. With her lyrics, I feel like she's capturing the same spirit, this desire and nostalgia and heartache and passion all wrapped up together at once, that's her Romantic energy to me."

Professor Mitchell looks up from the patch.

"You would love this piece that I sometimes give students to read, I didn't include it in our reading for this year's class because I wanted to focus more on the texts themselves, but it would really compliment the kinds of things I hear you talking about right now. It's…well I can't think of what it's called. I'll look for it and send it over to you tonight."

"Awesome! Wow, you're letting me take home a lot of goodies."

"Well, this is my favorite part of the job. I'll send you the article tonight. What's your university email?"

"Oh, well… I've been having a little trouble accessing that too recently. Maybe we can just find it later."

"I'm sorry all the university's technology is working against you right now."

"It's okay, I'm sure it'll get fixed soon. I'm excited to read that article. Now I'm sure you're really ready to get out of here."

"I will see you tomorrow in class, Lapis. If I find it, I'll bring it for you tomorrow."

"Awesome, see you then!"

Lapis wheels her bicycle down the hallway and down the narrow stairwell.

gorgeous light, such a gentle soul, if i could be that, if i could be that light, be that light when I'm her age, be that light for somebody when they hear me, be that light that reaches inside them and shines on the secrets, the hidden ones, and brings them out

Professor Mitchell remains in her office for another moment, looking out her window at the sky growing dark.

sat up here for 30 years, 30 autumns, and watched. What I want to know, more than anything else, is how the wind can stir up the leaves and trees, the air can grow cold, the sky grows dark and spreads itself over the city, and still it doesn't rain.

Lapis pedals through campus.

feels like it should rain tonight, the trees know it's coming, they smell it, feel it almost, feel it... like randell did

The wind begins rustling loudly through the trees as Lapis arrives at her apartment and loads the bicycle up the stairs. She rests it against the wall.

randell always knew when the first big rain would happen, said he could feel it, he'd watch the sky get dark, wind swirling around us, howling through the trees, scattering the dry leaves over the broken glass, and we'd listen as it came slowly, breathing together

Professor Mitchell emerges from Townsend Hall. She wraps her scarf around her neck.

why does it refuse to release itself, what's holding it back? why does it insist on restraining itself together tightly, withholding until the very last possible moment, when everything has become so desperate, that's what I'd like to know

Lapis unrolls her sleeping bag and lays down on the floor, staring at the ceiling.

and he'd say listen, it's coming softly, it's all breaking apart, hear that the sky's breaking apart

Lapis closes her eyes.

57

and i listened… and slowly, so slow at first, the sky begTan to fall over us in small pieces, tapping against the roof of my car, scattering itself widely over the lake

She turns onto her side and curls up inside the sleeping bag.

and we walked out under the dripping trees, walked softly through the shadows of those giant firs, and listened to the sky fall shattering against the lake, stirring it as each drop fell, as far as we could see

Randell notices the trees rustling in the wind through the front windows of the corner store. He leans heavily against the counter to take the strain off his back. He hears the group of middle school kids laughing from the other side of the store.

Jesus fuck only two more hours to go

He leans even farther forward to lessen the pressure on his lower back, pressing his body weight onto the counter.

two hours to go, an hour twice, just thirty minutes four times sure is windy out there

He hears something heavy fall to the floor and break across the store and the panicked hushes and laughter from the kids.

for fucks sake breaking shit

Before he has a chance to go inspect the damage, the group flies past him, sprinting through the aisles and out the door.

"Hey, get back here right now!" Randell yells after them. But they're gone before he can get around the counter. He walks slowly to the back of the store, to the refrigerated aisle, where he heard the crash. The floor of the aisle is covered, nearly end-to-end, in broken glass and spilled beer.

you've gotta be fucking kidding me… fucks sake

On the far end of the aisle he finds the limp six pack container of beer, itself covered in glass.

even middle schoolers are drinkin IPAs these days huh Jesus fucking Christ

He retrieves the mop bucket from the closet and begins mopping up the mess, collecting the brown broken glass in one place.

man the guys would love to see this, mopping up kids messes, pushing a broom at a corner store they would have a fucking riot they saw me now

He mops slowly in long sweeps of the mop.

they'd say hey look at randell lane pushin a broom not so big and strong now are ya lane...all tore up your hippie girlfriend broke up with you had to move to the city and mop up kids messes

When he finishes cleaning the aisle, he returns the mop bucket to the closet and walks back to the counter. The store is empty.

they'd say look at randell lane strongest kid in town carrying a fucking mop used to be so fucking cocky walking around town after the game on friday nights

The second hand of the clock on the wall clicks slowly.

they'd say look at randell lane came and beat our asses when we were messing with the special kids now he's pushin a mop

Randell tightens his fist until his knuckles turn white, the memory washes over him, absorbed in *that afternoon in the spring, cruising around with lapis like always, the blooming trees going wild all around the lake, that wide open sky so huge above the warm green hills, wrapped up in that little valley...driving over to the school just for fun, laughing and having fun then we saw those fucking guys out behind the school messin with the special kids, like what kind of person does that, how can you look at yourself, and Lapis stops the car and I rip out HEY WHATS GOIN ON OVER HERE get outta here rand*

*we're just messing around NO WHATS GOING ON OVER
HERE we're just playin around*

Randell feels the vein in his neck bulging.

*couldn't think I was so mad just blind fucking rage
couldn't see, heard Lapis yell leave those kids alone fucking
assholes, he calls back we're just teaching them how to catch
and he beams a ball at that poor kid right in the stomach*

He feels the sweat drip off his forehead.

*that's when I fucking lost it, can't even remember it I
was so mad just out of control threw that fucker to the ground
guys tried to pull me off but they couldn't, heard Lapis yelling at
me to stop but I couldn't stop what kind of person does that to
those poor kids can't even defend themselves, I guess those other
guys ran away and called the cops and I just wailed on that guy,
cursing and yelling and I saw the blood flying everywhere and
then there was blood on my hands*

He bends over the counter and rubs his temples.

*That's when I stopped, and it was all over my hands and
he wasn't moving anymore just still on the ground*

Randell looks down at his hands, trembling.

and I guess he still can't walk

He moves his hands to his temples and begins rubbing
them slowly.

*and I looked up and Lapis was crouched down with
those kids had her arms around those poor kids comforting them
and...and...she looked up at me like she didn't know me like she
was just horrified of me*

He squeezes his eyes shut.

*and everyone said the same thing why'd you handle it
that way? you know that'll follow you for the rest of your life,
why'd you hurt him so bad, you could have graduated and
maybe gone and played somewhere, why'd you throw that all
away? Was it worth it? kicked out of school, can't graduate,*

parents think you're some kind of monster, go live out on the street

He tries to breathe slowly.

and my question is this. what the fuck is your problem thinking I had any choice? my question is why wouldn't you have done the exact same thing? if you think I did the wrong thing then I don't see any difference between those assholes and you

Randell feels the anger flow through him in a strong current.

and she never looked at me the same

The bell above the door rings as a person enters the store. They shop around for a few minutes before bringing a bottle of wine to the counter. As Randell rings them out, they reach over to the small assortment of flowers and draw out a bundle of roses. Randell looks at the floral display closely.

When the night shift worker arrives, Randell walks to the back room and hangs his apron on a nail jutting out from the wall. He walks through the store, waves with one hand at the night shifter. As he pushes the glass door open, he stops for a moment and walks back into the store.

The night shifter looks up from her phone as he approaches the counter.

"Let me have one of these, I'll pay tomorrow when I come in."

He grabs a bouquet from the display.

"You can't do that," she says.

"Okay, just let me take a couple flowers then."

He plucks a couple small dahlias from a bouquet, ones that he hopes will match the wallpaper, and leaves into the cold night. He walks slowly down the street, protecting the flowers from the wind with his hands.

that smell in the air, even in the city you can smell it, but nothing like out there by the lake... won't be long now, tell you

61

*that not long at all, a couple days and it'll pour and pour like
you've never seen it*

He holds the flowers in both hands as he walks home,
wrapping the stems gently in his right hand, shielding them from
the wind with his left.

The sound of chairs and papers shuffling draws Nigel
out of his book. He looks up at the clock on the wall, high above
his desk in the reading room, and bolts suddenly from his chair.
He piles his books into his bag quickly, placing loose papers
inside the books, then throws his pens and crayons into the bag
on top of the books, zipping it up and fashioning it snugly on his
shoulders. Next, he turns towards the large roll of wallpaper
leaning against the side of his desk. He squats low and hoists it
up onto his left shoulder. He walks quickly through the reading
room and begins descending the stairs two at a time, bracing the
wallpaper with his hand.

He strides quickly across the ground floor, towards the
front entrance.

"Hey Nigel, leaving a little early tonight?" the custodian
calls from across the foyer. The custodian smiles and rests his
hands on his mop.

"Geez, where you goin with that roll of wallpaper?"

"Hey, Eric. Sorry, no time to talk tonight." He doesn't
slow down as he talks, walking directly towards the door.

"My roommate Randell just got off work and I need to
see him and show him this new wallpaper. I'll see you tomorrow
night I have a lot of important ideas…"

Nigel's voice trails off as he pushes the big front doors
of the library with his shoulder and leaves. He descends the stone
stairs quickly and continues down the walkway. The darkness
rests heavily over the campus. He passes under the oaks, the
branches swaying widely with the wind.

62

these are the emblems of the revelation experience, the moment of confession... intensity, passion, memory, desire

He feels the wind blow through his hair, he feels it run through his jacket, shirt, and across his chest.

to combine intensity, passion, memory, and desire, to press them together

He speeds up as he approaches the end of the walkway, where the row of scarlet oaks rises into the night from around the corner.

and at a moment of urgency, when the tension is at its greatest, these emblems dissolve

A gust of wind rolls through the trees. Nigel holds his wallpaper tighter.

everything disperses, the confession remains

Nigel turns the corner.

"Ow! Damn it!"

The impact knocks the wallpaper from his hands. He scrambles to pick it up before it unravels. As he reaches down he notices the man on his knees.

"Oh, I'm sorry are you okay? I didn't see you coming around the corner."

"Well you should be sorry!"

The man rubs his face.

"You need to watch where you're going with that thing."

The man slowly lumbers to his feet.

"Hey maybe you should stay down for a little longer, in case you're hurt."

"I'm not hurt damn it! Why do you think I'd be hurt? You think I'm soft?."

Nigel doesn't respond immediately.

"I... I don't know."

"Tell me. Do I look soft to you?"

The man finally rises to his feet and walks closer to Nigel.

63

"What is it? Do I look soft?"

"Well, if you are, it's okay. It's okay to be soft."

The man scoffs.

"That's a typical answer, that's how you all sound. I wonder sometimes if you guys even listen to yourselves. Undergrad punks. Think you know so damn much. But all you guys do is repeat stupid shit like that over and over."

The man takes another step closer. Nigel watches his eyes.

"Sir, I'm sorry I hit you with my wallpaper and upset you. It was an accident. I'm just trying to get home."

"You know I spend all day dealing with punks like you. I thought it's what I wanted to do with my life. I went to a good college and studied hard, got good grades. I loved learning. But guess what? That doesn't mean shit. It's not about learning. Know what you can do with a degree in sociology?"

"Lots of things."

"Wrong! You go to grad school or work at a fucking coffee shop. So I went to grad school, learned all about oppression and how everything's easier for me because I'm a white male. All that shit. Go home for fucking Christmas and dad would ask about my work and what do I say? What can I say to him? He's an investment banker and I take classes about male privilege."

"How about we sit down? Let's sit down."

Nigel gestures towards a nearby bench. The man smacks his hand away.

"And what did I do it for? To get a job making no money so I can deal with know it all punks like you. And all that shit my parents say, soft hours, read books and get paid, summers off. They say I don't even do any real work, don't add anything to the world."

"Let's sit down and talk for a little."

"Sure, let's do that."

The man grabs Nigel hard by the neck and pushes him onto the bench. He stands over him.

"Sir I know you're angry but let's not get violent. How about you just let me go home?"

"Nope. You're going to hear this. Somebody's going to hear my side for once. Because here's the thing. My parents are right, I don't add anything to the world. I'm making it worse. That's what they all told me right? That's what I was supposed to learn. That's the point of all this. Teach you that men are evil. You know that's what I should tell my dad. Hey dad thanks for spending all that money for me to learn that I make the world worse, and even more to train me to make it worse for everybody else."

Nigel rises from the bench.

"You matter, you don't..."

The man pushes him back onto the bench. He kneels down and looks Nigel in the eyes.

"But that's not enough for them. No way! That's not nearly enough. They can't stop at convincing me that I'm everything that's wrong with the world. They can't stop at just sticking me up there in front of all those whiny punks. And all they want to do is make me look stupid. That's not enough. Nope. They do all that, then tell me I'm not doing it the way they want. Isn't that great? They wait until five to tell me there's been a complaint filed against me and I need to get all these documents arranged. So I have to sit in that office until midnight and get all these documents together because somebody wants to complain."

Nigel tries to remain still. He feels the pain in his neck from where the man grabbed him.

"And they know they can do it because they think I'm soft. They think they can tell me what to do. And they're right. They control me. I'm a little fucking embarrassment of a person. I sit in a chair and answer emails. I let women tell me what to do,

65

my father thinks I'm a coward. And he's right. He's right. I am. But that doesn't matter. None of that matters. You know why?"

"No, I don't know why."

"Because it's not about doing the best you can. It's not about helping young people. It's not about learning. It's definitely not about expanding the body of human knowledge. None of that. You know what it's about?"

"What is it about?" Nigel whispers.

"It's about destroying the world. Destroying joy, destroying family, destroying everything that made this life worth living. And for what? So a few women can hide away in these buildings and pretend they're making the world a better place."

The man looks out into the night, over the dark shadows of the buildings. The branches waver above them. Nigel thinks very carefully.

"Do you have a safe place to stay tonight?"

"Just shut up."

The man watches the trees wave around the dark shadows of the buildings. Nigel chooses his words deliberately.

"Listen, you matter, and you're loved," he says as he leans forward.

"Shut the fuck up!" the man screams as he throws a punch at Nigel's face. Nigel falls from the bench and crumbles to the sidewalk.

"Oh, fuck, damn it, fuck," the man says as he backs away. He looks both ways down the street. There's no one around. He turns and walks away quickly, passing under the leaves of the scarlet oaks, and disappears behind them.

Nigel stirs after a few moments and lays on his back. He feels the wind blow across his body, and a dampness spreading across his face. He touches his cheek with his fingers and feels the blood.

randell help me

Randell enters the dark apartment.

he's still at the library, huh... probably having a good conversation with that custodian friend of his

Randell rests the flowers on the kitchen counter. He takes a large glass from the cupboard and fills it with water.

but he'll like to see these when he gets home, hope they... what did he call it... mesh. Hope they mesh with his wallpaper and the sunrise

Nigel attempts to stand after a few moments. The streetlight wavers and vibrates in front of him.

wow there's a light that's... that it's under the streetlight wow it is

He braces himself against the bench and waits for the dizziness to pass.

Randell takes a beer from the refrigerator. He drinks it quickly.

looks good to me at least, but i'm no good at stuff like this

He burps loudly and takes another beer from the refrigerator.

Nigel tries to stand without bracing himself against the bench.

randell please

He watches the red leaves circle through the darkness.

be here

He feels hot tears welling up in his eyes as he gathers the wallpaper off the ground, squeezing it to his chest, he takes a breath.

Randell tosses an empty can into the sink.

he's over there thinking about something important, all those ideas and philosophies he reads about... shit

He staggers to the bathroom with a beer in his hand. He drinks it quickly and sets it on the ground. He leans against the counter and stares into the mirror at his own eyes.

*i don't know anything about those things either, poetry
and that... all that stuff. but i could tell you anything you want
about pourin concrete*

He watches his eyes in the mirror.

*and i could tell you about the right thing, doing the right
thing, even when it's hard, even when everyone around thinks
you're wrong, even when they hate you and take everything
away*

He ambles into his room and collapses onto his bed.

*but you know what... i tried...they cant take that away,
she can say whatever she wants.. at least i fucking tried*

Nigel walks slowly down the sidewalk, squeezing the
wallpaper to his chest.

Thursday October 14th

Lapis rolls her sleeping bag tightly and sets it against the
wall. She pushes the milk crates carefully out of the way,
creating enough space for her routine. She lights a stick of
incense and nestles it on the milk crate under her guitar. She sets
a small paper plate on the floor to catch the ashes. She kneels on
the floor and sinks into child's pose. The light falls weakly
through her window, settling on a small square on the floor.
When she stretches back into downward facing-dog, the square
of light appears on her back, distorted by her spine. She holds the
position for a minute, feeling the stretch in her back and
hamstrings. She keeps her eyes closed. She breathes deeply.

She hears her phone buzz on the other side of the room.
She gently sets her knees on the ground before standing and
crossing the room to answer the call. She winces when she sees
the name on the screen. She lets the phone buzz in her hand
again. Then she answers it.

"Good morning, Susan."

68

There's a pause before a voice answers.

"I told you there's no smoking. That was the one thing you had to promise me."

"But I'm not smoking."

"The tenant in the next unit just called and woke me up to tell me they smell smoke...again."

"I was just burning some incense."

"Well, that's smoke. Come on, please, can you just not do it in the apartment? Go somewhere else and do it."

"I promise you; I'm not smoking. I'm just burning incense."

"Okay. But you realize it's not about what they smell. It's that they smell something coming from an empty unit. When I'm getting calls from people telling me there's weird smells coming from the unit that's supposed to be vacant, you see the position that puts me in?"

"Of course I understand that. I'm sorry. I was just trying to make it feel more comfortable. More like home."

"I know, but you gotta help me out here. Why don't you just move back to town and stay with us."

"You know I'm not doing that."

"But why not? What's so special about the city? You need a freakin' air mask to walk down the street. Hippies everywhere. I guess you like that sort of thing. That's your crowd. Not us, the only reason I hold onto those apartments is the money's so good, college kids pay anything. That almost makes up for the hassle."

"I won't burn incense anymore."

"Why don't you come out to the orchard and visit us. You always loved the colors this time of year."

"I'm sorry, I can't."

Susan doesn't say anything.

"I'm sorry about the incense. I really appreciate you letting me stay here until I can get things figured out."

69

"Come out and visit us this weekend. Come to church, it'll be good for you."

"I just can't go back there right now. I just really can't. But I will someday, I'll come stay with you and work on the orchard again. Maybe in the summer. I just need some time to be here around people like me and forget everything."

"Oh, you're not still blaming yourself for what that boy did are you? You know there was nothing you could do."

"Let's not get into it."

"Is that what all this is about? That's why you convinced me to let you stay in that crummy apartment no one will rent? You think it's your fault he hurt that boy so bad?

"Susan…"

"Well, it's not. You can't fix men like that, everyone told you that. Men like that, those tortured souls. Hurt that sweet boy so bad."

"That sweet boy you refer to was terrorizing kids with special needs. Let's just drop it okay?"

"Oh sweetie, you still believe that story? I've known that family my whole life. They sit in the pew in front of us every Sunday. He wouldn't do anything like that, bullying those special kids, no way. And besides, the security footage didn't even show anyone else there."

"Susan, it's not a story, I was there. I saw it. I know what happened. And I don't want to get into it. Please, is there anything else you wanted to tell me?"

Susan doesn't respond. Lapis feels her heart beating quickly.

"I'm sorry, I won't burn incense anymore."

"Take care of yourself down there. Don't let anyone take advantage of you. You'll come visit us out here? Say you will."

"I'll come visit, I promise. I'll pick peaches all summer, I'll do whatever you need me to do. I just need to get things

70

figured out. Don't worry about me, I already made a new friend."

"We love you, Lapis. Jesus loves you, too."

"Thanks Susan, tell everyone I love them. I'll talk to you later."

Lapis places the phone on the ground and buries her face in the wall, breathing deeply. The light falls weakly through the window.

imagine me going back there, can you even imagine that?

She presses her forehead against the wall and squeezes her eyes shut.

where they stare and stop and turn their heads, where they idle their trucks and talk to each other out the window, where those guys at the gas station watch you get into your car and call out gross things

She tries to slow down her breathing.

and they get together in those fields and congratulate each other on being pious Christians, wax poetic on their small-town values, community, safety, and shake their heads and frown at the ones who don't fit in

She inhales slowly.

and their boys hurt each other but they don't think about it

She rubs her eyes and steps away from the wall. She runs her hands under the cold water.

because anytime their sweet boys do something that might disturb their perfect world they drown it in the lake, sink it all the way to the cold bottom and never speak of it

She feels her hands grow cold under the water.

but they didn't let randell breathe in that town, even when he was gone they went on whispering to themselves in the parking lots, on their front porches, whispering and shaking their head, that self-righteous look in their eyes, that holy glance over the big lake, that calm pride in the strength and endurance of their fragile fragile world

She shuts off the faucet. She dries her hands on her pants.

i'm not saying he should have done it, i've never said that

She sees the phone light up on the ground out of the corner of her eye.

i just wish, wish he could have...

She bends and picks the phone up from the ground. She opens the text message.

mandy wants to know if I still want to read after class today, yes of course I do, I wonder if she's been to that little garden

She types her response carefully and sends it, placing her phone on the ground again. She sits on the floor and leans back against the wall. After a few moments, she takes Professor Mitchell's copy of the Romantic anthology from her bag. She stretches out on the floor, situating the book squarely within the faint slab of light trailing in faintly through the window. She flips to the John Keats section of the anthology and turns carefully until she reaches *Ode to a Nightingale*, where Professor Mitchell's hand-written notes sprawl wildly across the page.

Mandy watches Lapis' response appear on her screen. She hesitates.

i could say like Okay see you later! or maybe something like awesome! See you this afternoon! Or I don't respond at all

She stares at the message. She hears the water in the bathroom stop.

how about cool! See you soon!

She feels the stirring in her stomach, the butterflies dancing.

or how about can we call it a date? and i'll bring the tea this time, just please look at me like you did, holding the peach, you don't have to call me pretty, just smile like you did

She hears the door open in the hallway and Jess' footsteps approaching the door. She locks her phone and places it on the ground beside the bed just before Jess enters the room.

"You aren't going to class today?" Jess asks as she hangs her towel over a chair.

"Are you?"

"Of course I'm going. I'm still entitled to receive my education even though I ask questions the instructor doesn't like."

"That's not what I mean. I just didn't think you would want to go today after what happened last time."

Jess doesn't respond. She dresses quickly.

"And what's the rush anyway? It's only, what, 9?"

Mandy reaches for her phone to clarify; she stops herself just before she picks it up.

"I told you yesterday I wanted to get to campus earlier today. I need to print some things before class. You don't have to come with me, I just thought you wanted to."

Mandy imagines a message appearing on her screen, the name flashing brightly in front of her.

"Mandy?"

"Yes?"

"Are you coming?"

"I don't think so."

"Why not?"

"I just don't feel like it. And I need to get caught up on my reading."

Jess takes her jacket from the coat hanger.

"Can you please text me about what you're doing today?"

"I will, I'm sorry about Tuesday."

73

"It's just already been such an exhausting week, and these are the times that I really need you to be there for me. When everyone's against me I need you to be there."

"I know. I'm sorry."

"I'll see what I can get done today. Then this weekend I just want to relax and not think about any of it."

"I want to go to that house show tomorrow. The one my friend invited us to."

"Does that sound like relaxing? Standing in a cramped house with sweaty white guys?"

"I don't think it'll be like that."

"We'll talk about. I have to go. Please text me."

"I will."

Jess gathers her books from the table in the living room. She closes her computer and slips it into the bag. From the bedroom, Mandy hears the door shut firmly. She reaches for her phone on the ground and pulls up Lapis' messages. She stares at the letters, the name on the screen.

why would she stop me and bring me my pen, just to be nice? because she's a kind person? but then why would she ask me to go hang out with her right away, and why would she bring peaches, and why would she look at me like she wants to make out in the grass

She sits up and turns to the window. She parts the curtains and lets the soft light fall into the room.

and why tell me about her music, about how she wants her voice to be raw desire, she wants it to run through me and light up every nerve inside me, she wants to know my secret

She falls back to the bed and stares at the ceiling.

why ask me to hang out again? why? just to be friendly? because she's new to campus and wants someone to read with? why choose me?

She grabs her phone again.

i could tell her right now, i could tell her that i need to get away, that this is my last chance, that we could leave together right now, leave and go and get away never look back

A message appears on the screen. Mandy feels a shock surge through her body. Then a picture appears below the message.

she says she's trying to get caught up before class today. that looks like a different edition of the anthology, and that's a lot of annotation

Mandy hops off the bed and digs through her bag until she finds her copy of the anthology. She types a response quickly.

how about what a coincidence me too! excited for class!

She deletes the message.

come on something good, come on.... that's a beautiful edition, looking forward to hear what you think about it-- does that work?

She deliberates for another moment, then presses send.

gone. sent.

She drops the phone on the bed, walks to the bathroom, and turns on the shower.

is it too much to ask for these guys to not block the entire sidewalk?

Jess passes the group widely on their left and speeds up when she returns to the right side of the sidewalk. She strikes the ground hard with her boots, crunching leaves with every step. The sidewalk flows into the campus from the old neighborhood on its east side. As the sidewalk winds into the heart of campus, it passes under the shade of several of the oldest white oaks. The oaks spread themselves over the lawn and keep the walkers hidden from the other side of the trees.

frat guys taking up too much space. Surprised they're even awake… probably late for their 9 am

Jess walks quickly under the white oaks. The walkway winds through lawns and near buildings before easing into the busy center of campus, joining 7th street near the front staircase of Anthony Hall. Jess climbs the stairs and enters the building.

still cold and dusty

The door to Professor Anderson's office is closed when she reaches the top floor. She taps lightly on the door.

not here yet

Jess checks her phone.

not here at 9:30, well damn it

She leans her back against the wall.

how is it already stuffy up here? it's so cold downstairs

She hears the sound of steps in the stairwell. Then Professor Anderson appears at the end of the hallway.

"Hi Jess, sorry I'm late. It was kind of a hectic morning."

"That's totally okay. It's good to see you."

"Come on into the office."

Professor Anderson opens her office door and sets her things down on the floor.

"Sorry again about making you wait. Things were a little messy with my kid this morning."

"Oh don't worry, thanks for meeting me. I just wanted to check and see how things went yesterday."

"Let's find out. We sent him the notice around five yesterday. He might not have received the notice; in which case he would need to get in touch with him more directly to request all the materials. But let's see."

Professor Anderson makes several clicks before opening the page.

"Oh wow."

"What is it?"

"Well, it's all here. He submitted it late last night. And he agreed to our request to meet as soon as possible. It looks like I'll be meeting with him tomorrow morning at 8 A.M. over in the conference room on the other end of the hall."

"And what about me?"

"What do you mean?"

"Will I get a chance to voice my concerns to the people in the department?"

"Well, I'm acting as sort of a liaison. I'm representing your concerns with the other department admin."

"So I don't get to be at the table."

"Well... we just want to minimize the amount of stress..."

"Julie. This whole thing is causing me stress. But if there's going to be a meeting about his incompetence then I want to be there."

"I understand that. It's just our policy to limit these meetings to the faculty. We can't have undergraduates barging in and confusing the matter."

"What do you mean 'confusing the matter'?"

"This is a good thing, Jess. He's going to be held up to scrutiny and we're going to take your criticism very seriously in our evaluation."

"And then everything stays the same."

"Not necessarily. He'll likely be asked to revamp his course to include a more diverse array of perspectives. That's what we wanted, right?"

"You're going to ask him to make his syllabus look less like a copy of who's who in white academia and just trust that all the problems will just go away?"

"He'll still have to through our regular instructional quality protocols."

Jess stands up and moves towards the door.

"Wait, Jess. Don't leave. What's wrong? How have I upset you?"

"He thinks that MLK was a political moderate who just wanted everyone to get along. How do you think you can fix that frame of mind? You can't."

"I know this has all been so frustrating for you. But this is just an institutional procedure. We can't fire people because one undergraduate student complained about his handling of a subject."

"You've got to be fucking kidding me."

"This is a good thing."

"His handling of a subject? It's not his handling of a subject, it's that his views are totally anti-justice and miss the point about everything to do with the history of activism. These aren't just differences of opinion; this is about your willingness to protect your students from violence."

"We take your input very seriously Jess."

"And to be honest, it's exhausting having to say this over and over again. Do you care about protecting vulnerable students from someone who can't see past his own privilege?"

"Of course we care, and we value your input."

"Yeah. I got that part. Let me just ask you this. Why study critical theory? Why get so deep into these institutional critiques and models of equity in education? Why spend your life doing this work if, when presented with an opportunity to actually change something, you're just going to fold and follow the policy?"

"I don't know what to tell you, Jess. It's our policy. These are just the rules we have to play by."

"Playing by the rules. I'm told that's how the voting rights act was passed. You must get your history from Mark Whiteside."

"Don't attack me, Jess. We've known each other for a few years, but you still need to treat me with respect."

"Why is it disrespectful to point out that you're falling into the same trap as everybody else? Why do I have to care more about protecting people's feelings than I do about advocating for people's actual fucking lives?"

"You're certainly allowed to be upset, but don't get angry with me when I'm the one that's going into that meeting tomorrow to advocate for you."

Jess turns and leaves the office, walking quickly down the hall and into the stairwell.

unfuckingbelievable. you have a chance to really make a difference, to use your intellectual training to help bring justice and all you want to do is sit in your office and sign paperwork. I thought you said you hated it up there, you really wanted to do the real work of being an academic, but that was a lie

She descends the stairs with powerful steps, clenching her fists.

literally what's the point? what's the point of being here and studying and doing all this work if when faced with a situation of obvious injustice you just retreat back into the status quo?

Jess reaches the bottom of the staircase and crosses the landing into the main hallway on the first floor. She stops to fill her water bottle from the fountain. She watches the water pour into the metal bottle.

when you're just going to retreat into the status quo, as if real human lives aren't on the table

As the water brims to the top of the bottle, Jess releases her hand from the faucet. A door opens behind her. She screws on the lid of her bottle.

when you're just going to retreat into the status quo like the university is just the world's most expensive game of charades

She turns and finds Mark Whiteside standing behind her. He looks up from his phone and his eyes grow wide.

"Jess... I... good morning."

Jess opens her mouth. She feels a surge of anger run through her. She squeezes the cap tightly to the bottle.

"I'm just going to get some water before class starts," Whiteside says as he steps forward to the fountain. He presses the button and holds his plastic bottle under the water.

Jess opens her mouth again. She takes a breath. She turns away from the fountain and walks down the hallway.

you're incompetent and don't deserve a job at this...you're so incompetent and lazy and stupid

She walks down the hallway, feeling her face growing warm as she passes under the large windows, through the columns of dust falling slowly through the weak light.

and why would you submit to the status quo when you have a chance to really change something, to bring some justice

She pushes the door open and steps out into the morning. The sunlight settles softly on the lawn in front of Anthony hall.

and i'm not going to let it happen

She walks slowly up 7th street, floating among the crowds of students hurrying to their ten o'clock lectures. She chooses a bench underneath a pair of small maple trees, their leaves flashing yellow in the soft morning light.

She sits still for a minute, watching the last few students scurry into buildings up and down 7th street.

is it just a joke and i missed it? are they just pretending to care? do they just want to talk about it, sit together and talk about it and never do anything. who cares how many books you've published, how many panels you've sat on, how revolutionary you sound in your fucking article...how does any of that matter?

She sits still on the bench, her eyes frozen on the lawn unfolding before her.

am I the only one? why... why is it my job to stand up to him. why should i stay there and stand up to him

80

She reaches into her bag and brings out her phone.

is that fair?

She selects Mandy's name and presses the call button. She brings the phone to her face.

no, it's incredibly unfair

The phone rings in her ear. It rings again. She feels the tears balancing in her eyes.

no fucking way, no FUCKING way

She hears Mandy's automated voice mail message in her ear. She drops the phone in her lap and presses her hands into her eyes.

and when everything's falling apart, she's not there for me. why? because i made one mistake? so i'm just a terrible person because i made one mistake? because i got lonely and got a stupid boy to pay attention to me? sure, i did that. but i've been great for her and i've always been there for her, always

The wind rustles calmly through the maple trees above Jess' head. A yellow leaf falls, spinning slowly through the air, coming to rest on the sidewalk. The dark clouds pass slowly over the hills to the east, swelling over the green covered tops of the mountains.

Randell awakes to the sound of quaking in his ear.

aw hell

He fumbles out of bed searching for the sound. He digs through his sheets, tosses them aside, and rifles through a pile of garbage on the floor next to his bed.

where is that fucking thing

He pushes an empty box of beer away and clears an empty space around his bed. The loud quaking continues.

good lord

He follows the quaking with his hands, searching under the pile of dirty clothes nestled behind the bed.

come on where are you

81

He sifts through the stack of empty beer cans behind the bed, searching for the sound.

Jesus i gotta toss some of these empties

He finds a leg belonging to the pair of jeans he wore to work. He pulls on the leg, finding it tangled among the other articles of clothing. He pulls harder until the knot unfurls and the jeans come free from the mess of shirts and underwear.

He digs through the pockets of the jeans until he wrestles out the quaking phone and turns the alarm off.

nothing like nabbin those birds over the lake in the fall...just last year...but they never sound that annoying

Randell opens his door to the living room and into the bathroom. He collects his empty cans from the floor and brings them to the kitchen. He gathers the cans on the kitchen counter and the ones from the sink and drops them all in a large plastic bag.

no Nigel yet huh.... geez must be on a bender over there. i guess he said sometimes he stays there till lunch...can't imagine how you read anything for that long

Randell takes the bag of cans down the stairs and out into the alley. He feels the cool morning air on his bare chest. He grabs the opening of the bag firmly in his hand and spins it before tossing it into the large dumpster in the alley. He hears the cans spill out of the bag as it bangs against the side of the dumpster. He walks back inside.

but i guess you could say the same thing about hunting. why would anyone want to sit out in the cold at 5am and wait for a bird to fly over. wasted plenty of hours staring out at the lake those mornings...just stare at the lake for hours and sink my eyes down into it

He climbs the stairs and walks back into the apartment.

and start to see funny things sometimes, as the sky would turn from black to purple, and the trees rise out from the blackness and loom over the lake like dark scraggly statues

He walks into the kitchen and sees the flowers in their vase.

and the water's real calm, and it's got this funny look like it's changing colors, that purple sky reflecting on it, then the breeze starts up and the purple sky lake ripples from the one bank all the way to those huge dark Firs on the other side

He leans back against the wall and stares at the flowers in the window.

and if you stare long enough into the ripples you see them flash like broken purple crystals, shimmering and flashing and something about being awake so early, being out there in the trees, you felt like the flashes were little secrets about the future or the past maybe... but i swore those flashes were telling me something, something i had no right to know, something i had no reason to know, but once i knew it i could never let it go

Randell feels his back growing sore from standing. He walks back into the living room and sits on the couch.

and it's the kind of thing you can't explain to anybody. they wouldn't understand, especially out there, those guys would never understand, and Lapis...i guess she already knew it

Randell softens his back into the cushion.

those flowers, gotta admit they look good on the windowsill, tilted just like that in the light, i guess i got lucky with that

He relaxes into the soft couch, closing his eyes.

come to think of it, i don't really remember setting them on the windowsill... no i didn't, i just set them on the counter so Nigel could put them where he wanted, must've got too drunk

Randell grunts as he stands up from the soft couch. He walks back to the kitchen and leans against the kitchen counter.

but no i remember putting them right on the counter. that way Nigel could put them how he wanted them

The soft morning light falls on the yellow pedals of the Dahlia.

he must've come back and done it himself

Randell stares at the Dahlias.

and now he's off again like always...always goin somewhere with a new idea

Randell notices a small corner of white paper peeking out from underneath the glass. He reaches for it and pulls on it gently, bracing the glass with his other hand. He unfolds the piece of paper.

oh but he left me a note

Randell turns away from the window to get a better look at the note.

rand:

I've encountered a man or demon I did not understand. He was afraid and he hurt me. I've gone to fix it, but I don't know how long it will take or how long I'll be gone. Take care of the wallpaper while I'm gone. Your flowers compliment them so well. Please understand. I have to save everything before it's too late. with love

n+1

Randell reads the note quickly several times. He feels a bead of sweat growing on his forehead.

oh Jesus. shit. damn it. damn it.

He hurries into his room and pulls on the pair of jeans from his bed and a shirt from the broken knot. He grabs his leather jacket from the floor. He folds the piece of paper and places it in the pocket of his jeans. He disturbs a group of birds pecking for crumbs on the ground as he bursts through the front door and into the alley.

Mandy clears the steam from the mirror with her towel. A thin layer of fog appears over her face just as she finishes wiping the mirror. She watches herself underneath the layer of fog. She tries to ignore the turning in her stomach.

Lapis places Professor Mitchell's anthology in her bag gently. She extinguishes her stick of incense.

Mandy watches the steam reclaim the mirror, rising slowly over the space she cleared with her towel, her face disappears behind the fog. She closes her eyes.

Lapis ties her flannel around her waist. She carries her bike down the staircase.

With her eyes closed, Mandy imagines the sky *hanging heavy black over us, wandering slowly up the mountain behind her, closed in by the fog seeping in over our shoulders, the blanket of sinking softly under our feet, watching her hair reflect the moonlight,*

Lapis pedals slowly up the street. She scans the sky briefly, noticing the clump of gray clouds congregating over the eastern hills.

Mandy feels the hot air in the bathroom wash over her.

stopping to rest under a fern bush, drinking wine secretly in the damp forest, sinking, sinking into her arms.

Lapis slows down as she reaches the intersection across from the southern entrance to the university. She watches the clouds stacking up over the mountain.

Mandy wraps the towel around herself and walks back to the bedroom.

the soft glow of her eyes mixing with the strange dark pulsing of the forest

When the light turns green, Lapis pedals through the intersection and veers over to the sidewalk, climbing a slight incline, and dips into the hedge.

Mandy gets dressed and gathers her books.

and the pulsing comes from nowhere, or at least I can't tell you where it is

Lapis rides the brakes through the hidden corridor, easing slowly into the garden.

Mandy stops at the door and waits.

85

but it's a whispering pulse, a quiet whisper rising from the depths of the forest, a strange murmuring, sink deeper into her arms

She closes the door behind her as she leaves.

With the bike hidden between the bushes, Lapis proceeds through the garden and out from under the trees into the soft light of the day. She grabs her phone from her pocket and types a message.

Mandy walks through the quiet neighborhood. She feels her phone vibrate gently in her pocket. She feels a jolt of surprise run through her when she sees Lapis' name appear on the screen.

I got to campus a little early. Are you out of your other class? Would you like to meet up before Romanticism?

Mandy feels her heart thump in her chest. She stops in the middle of the sidewalk as she responds to the message.

Lapis sees Mandy's text appear on her screen.

that sounds great! (: I'm almost to campus. Shall I meet you in front of the library?

Mandy waits for Lapis to respond.

that smiley face was a bad idea, such a bad idea okay here she said amazing I'll see you soon.

Lapis finds an empty bench in front of the library. She takes a deep breath.

Mandy walks quickly towards campus, crossing the intersection and cutting across a parking lot.

she wants to see you, she wants to hang out with you, it's okay, you're okay

As she approaches the library, Mandy spots Lapis sitting on a bench, she tries to settle the turning in her stomach.

Lapis lets her breath out slowly. She turns just as Mandy approaches.

Mandy walks quickly towards the bench. She sees Lapis turn towards her, lifting her head.

Their eyes meet as Mandy walks up to Lapis' bench.

"Hey! You made it!" Lapis calls, rising from the bench.

"Hey! Hi!...how are you?"

"I'm great, it's good to see you. How was your class?"

"It was... well I didn't go this morning. It was kind of a weird... I just didn't go."

"Is everything okay?"

"Oh yeah, everything's okay. It's just not a very good class."

"How so?"

"Our instructor is a little disorganized and not very...he's just not very good at teaching."

"That's too bad. That could be a really cool class."

"It really could."

Mandy watches the soft light fall through Lapis' hair. A breeze stirs the leaves at their feet. They're silent for a moment.

"You picked a nice spot here," Mandy says.

"I have an even nicer spot to show you, maybe you've already seen it before, it's this little garden behind the library."

"No, I've definitely never seen it before. I didn't know there was anything behind the library except trees and then the road."

"That's how it looks, but just right back there." Lapis points to the clump of bushes and trees on the side of the building.

"Right through there, there's a little path that leads to this open space that must have been a garden at some point and the university decided to not maintain it and seal it off from the sidewalks. I found it by accident a few weeks ago. I thought we could do our reading there after class. It has a sort of Keatsian atmosphere."

"That would be amazing. Let's do it."

"We could even go check it out now if you wanted, class doesn't start for another 20 minutes."

Mandy strains her eyes to see deeper into the bushes, to make out the faint trace of a path.

"We don't want to miss any part of a Lydia Mitchell lecture, that's for sure, I've just been so excited to show this place to someone" Lapis says with a smile.

"Yeah let's do it, but you'll have to lead the way."

"You'll think you're in the middle of nowhere, like you're in the middle of the woods."

The walkway runs under the brick facade of the library, jogging off slightly around the patch of trees and bushes. Mandy and Jess follow the walkway in the shade of the library, past the stone staircase. They pause when they reach the bushes.

"Now see this little path, it's overgrown, but see how it runs off down there into those trees?" Lapis points her finger to the ground, tracing the path through the bushes.

"No, I still don't see it." Mandy says.

"Yeah, it's hard to spot, especially with the light the way it is, no shadows. That's why no one goes there."

Lapis turns to look for the sun hidden among the clouds blanketing the sky. She notices the clump of gray clouds spreading out wider over the hills. She pans her eyes across the sea of students heading to their noon classes.

"Okay, you can follow me, I'll…."

Lapis trails off abruptly. Mandy looks up from the bushes at Lapis. Her eyes are fixed forward Her body is rigid.

"Are you okay?"

"I…I think I… oh wow okay, it's him."

"Who? Who is it?"

Lapis turns to Mandy, her face ghostly white.

"I just saw my ex-boyfriend," she says. Mandy notices the alarm in her voice.

"Where? Did he see you?"

"I think so."

"Is that okay? Are you safe?"

"Yeah, I'm safe. I just haven't seen him in... a long time. Do you see someone walking towards us?"

Mandy looks out over the lawn in front of the library. Suddenly, she notices a large man moving quickly towards them.

"I think so. He's big and he's wearing a leather jacket."

"That's him. Oh wow, okay. I'm...okay we can do this. Can you stay here with me? When he gets over here?"

"Of course. Yeah, of course. He's..."

"Thank you, you're the best. Is he.?"

"Lapis is that you?"

Mandy watches Lapis' eyes grow large for a fraction of a second before she whirls towards the voice. Randell wipes the sweat from his forehead.

"Lapis...Wha...what are you doing here?" he asks.

"I go to school here."

"You do? But how did you... I'm sorry I can't get into any of this right now, I'm in the middle of something really important."

He doesn't walk away.

"What are you doing here? And... why are you so sweaty?"

"Well I'm in a helluva hurry, a big hurry, I'm looking... oh man, this is a mess... I think something really bad is going on and I'm trying to figure out what to do."

"What's going on? Are you hurt? What is it?"

"No, it's not me, it's my roommate. Jesus, this is really a grease fire of a conversation, I'm sorry for walking over here I better just go."

"No, stay and tell us about it, if you can. Maybe we can help you."

Mandy watches Randell's big hands shake as he wipes them across his forehead, smearing the sweat across his face. She remains silent.

89

"Okay, so I have a roommate here in town. He's a super smart little guy and I think he's hurt, and I can't find him, don't know where he is, he left this note, I'm just kind of panicking here."

"Well, let's just settle down for a second and talk about it, okay?"

Mandy notices the change in Lapis' voice, a tone she hasn't heard before, a focus and seriousness which surprises her.

"Okay. That's a good idea. I just...everything's just really weird right now. This is, how are you a student here?"

Mandy watches Randell clear the hair away from his eyes and look at Lapis. She watches his lips tremble.

"Let's focus on one thing at a time. We'll figure out where your roommate is and we'll find him, okay. He'll be all right. Take some slow breathes. Nice and slow."

"Yeah, your meditation stuff isn't gonna work for me right now. I need to find him."

"Well if you take some breathes then you'll be in a better headspace to make the right decision."

Lapis turns to face Mandy.

"I can't go to class today; can you give Lydia my best for me. I think I'm going to take him somewhere and try to figure this out."

Mandy feels the sinking feeling return in her stomach as she watches them shuffle over to the bench and sit down. She watches Randell put his head in his hands. Lapis places her hand on his shoulder. Mandy turns away and begins down the walkway towards Townsend Hall, the ache sinking deeper in her stomach.

so this is what I do, I walk away and leave her there right when things get difficult and awkward, I walk away...and go sit in class and think about her, go home and imagine her walking next to me

She stops.

but I don't have to, I really don't have to, I don't have to walk away,

She turns around and walks back quickly towards the library, breaking into a light jog as she approaches the bench. She finds them just as they were a minute ago.

"Maybe my house would be a good place to kind of get things figured out. It's close by. Would that help?"

Randell looks up from his hands. Lapis starts up from the bench quickly.

"That's a great idea, Mandy! Do you think Jess would be alright with that?"

"Of course!"

Lapis turns back to Randell.

You should come with us and you can tell us more about it in a calmer, less chaotic space, and then we'll make a plan."

Randell hesitates for a moment. He glances up at Mandy, then back to Lapis.

"I don't know... I appreciate it, Mandy was your name right? I appreciate that gesture, but I just don't see how that helps me find him."

"You can't just run all around town looking for him." Lapis squats down and meets him at eye-level.

"Come with us, we'll talk about it and make a calm, mindful decision. This is the right thing."

He lets out a slow sigh.

"Okay. I'll come. But I don't wanna see the sun go down with him out there somewhere."

Randell rises slowly from the bench; he grunts as he straightens his back.

Mandy notices Lapis wince slightly as she watches him rise from the bench.

They walk together past the overgrown path back up the walkway out of the campus. After a few moments, Mandy attempts to break the silence.

"Look at those clouds, it looks like we'll finally get some rain."

"Not today," Randell says flatly. "Not yet."

Mandy keeps her head down the rest of the walk.

jess won't like this if she gets home, but she can't tell me what to do, it's my house too

Randell feels the dull pain in his back pulse with every step.

Jesus this sure is a shit show...dumpster fire, who would have thought now i'm walking around with lapis and.... her friend i guess. but why'd she say she's a college student, and that friend, something weird about all of it

Lapis watches the gray clouds spread out away from the hills, mixing into the fabric of the white overcast sky. She keeps her eyes on the dark clouds dispersing from over the hills into the valley.

and he was just there in the crowd, I know I saw him first, a head taller than everyone else and just so out of place, he was there looking all around for his friend, and somehow he turned and saw me, there on the edge of the trees, and his back still hurts from the crash, and he saw me in the crowd

Jess watches students file slowly past the glass window from her seat at the Presto cafe. The students cross the street under the row of scarlet oaks in large droves, pouring out from behind the trees and dispersing in every direction. The largest branch of the stream continues down 7th street, past the glass window of the Presto cafe. Jess swirls the coffee in her mug.

there they go

The espresso machine whirs quietly behind her. Across the cafe, a pair of students tap quickly on their keyboards.

going back home to repair themselves

Jess watches the students as they pass the window, an unceasing stream.

going home to study or cry or both

A small bell rings weakly as the door swings open.

and they're going into debt for this, unbelievable debt, to take their classes on autopilot, skim over books that took years to write, skim them to get a sentence for their bullshit paper, turn it in with last night's beer still on their breath

The wood floors creak.

and the professors sit up in those offices and click through forms and the administration sits up even higher and cashes their checks

The floor shakes slightly when he sets his roll of wallpaper on the floor. Jess turns away from the window.

well, that's not what I would bring to a coffee shop

He sets his elbow on the roll and examines the chalkboard menu hanging above the counter. Jess turns back to her coffee.

and still no text from Mandy

She hears the person with the wallpaper order at the counter.

it's time for a serious talk with her

She hears a loud slam and feels the floor shake near her feet. She turns to see the roll of wallpaper flat on the floor next to her. She looks up at the back of the person standing at the counter. His head is turned up to read the menu. She opens her mouth to speak, but hesitates. She turns her eyes back to the wallpaper on the ground.

wonder whose grandma he's bringing that to...what kind of bird is that, small little tan bird

When Nigel turns from the counter, he notices his wallpaper lying on the floor.

"Thanks for watching this," he says quietly.

"Sorry, I wasn't sure if I should pick it up or not."

"That's okay, gravity won that round. Do you like it?"

"What do you mean? The wallpaper?"

"Yeah, what do you think about it?

"I'm not sure. I guess I could see it working for some people."

"Yes!"

Jess jumps at Nigel's loud burst of excitement.

"Sorry," he says, "That was just such a great way of putting it. I really believe that. It works for some people. It works for some people."

Nigel glances at the ceiling.

"It works for some people."

Jess stares back down into her coffee.

that's a terrible cut under his eye, and it looks infected

"Does it work for you?" Nigel asks, without taking his eyes off the ceiling.

"Um... I don't know."

he's spent some nights outside

She looks again at the tan birds floating in the blue background.

"I don't mean to disturb your peace with these questions," Nigel says quickly, "I just get excited about it."

"No, it's okay. I don't think I like it, but maybe someone else would."

She smiles up at Nigel, who is still staring straight at the ceiling.

"What did you order?"

"Nothing."

"Would you like to sit down?"

His eyes snap back down to Jess.

94

"Of course!"

He picks up the wallpaper from the ground and leans it gently against the glass window before sitting down.

"Do you need a coffee, or anything like that?"

"No, caffeine's no good for me, I won't sleep for weeks if I have any."

Jess glances over at the wallpaper leaning against the window.

"So are you doing a project with that?"

"Absolutely!"

Nigel taps his fingers against the table. Then he folds them together and presses them tightly against his chest, trying to keep them still.

"Yes, I'm engaged in a very unstable project at the moment."

"Why is it unstable?"

"It's changing rapidly. Almost too quickly to keep up. And the techniques and practices are changing just as fast as the project itself. Just when you've brought everything close to you, packed it all together, it just explodes and disperses, dispersing into infinitesimal parts of wholes."

"I'm not sure I follow. What's changing?"

"The project. And the techniques. The parts."

"Right."

"Are you involved in any projects?"

"I... yes I am."

"So you know."

"What do I know?"

"How hard it is to just finish them."

"Yeah, I guess that's the hard part."

"You get so far along into it, and the finish line is changing the whole time, it's receding."

receding

"And then you look back and the start line isn't even where it was when you started. Then you look at yourself and you aren't even the same as when you started."

it's receding

"And then you take a second to figure out where you are, and it's not the same project anymore. You're somewhere else. And it's getting dark."

Nigel looks out the window. Jess stares at the table.

receding into a future i can't see

"Just a couple days ago, I had a moment where I brought it all together, a whole system of how my pieces fit together. Then something happened last night, and all those pieces got broken. So I started trying to understand that instability, and why all my pieces break apart into fragments when I try to put them together. And that's still what I'm doing."

"Well, it sounds like you're making progress."

"Progress, well... I'm talking too much, do you want to tell me about your project?"

"I guess I have a few. My program keeps me busy with little research papers and things like that, school projects, but what I really want to do, my real project, is support activist efforts through education. I try to gear my college work towards that bigger goal, sometimes it works."

"Projects operating within bigger projects."

"I'm Jess, by the way."

"It's a privilege to meet you, Jess."

She waits for a moment for him to introduce himself. He looks out the window.

"I wanted to ask," she continues after a long few seconds, "what kind of bird is that on the wallpaper?"

Nigel turns back to her and squeezes his eyes shut for a second, then opens them.

"It's a nightingale."

96

"Hm. I don't think I've ever seen one of those in person."

Nigel grins.

"They're ephemeral. I don't think they always exist. I think they appear selectively at moments of... heightened intensity, and then they disappear."

"Interesting take."

he needs something for that cut

"But that's just the basic quality of the universe, right? Fleeting, fleetingness. I really thought I had that all figured out, until last night."

"What happened to shake that certainty?"

"I'm talking too much. Do they have kombucha here?"

He turns back to the menu hanging from the ceiling.

"Maybe, I don't know."

She scans the cut closely, following it around his eye.

"Did something bad happen last night?"

"How can they not have any? Not even some that they keep in a jar under the sink?"

"Do you need something for the cut under your eye?"

"I love your project."

"What?"

"Do you have a favorite romantic poet?"

"Wait a second."

"Jess, we need your project."

"I'm getting lost here."

"We need your project. Jess. You have to do it."

"Do what?"

"I know it's not easy and there's a million things in your way, but you just have to…"

He presses his hands together until they turn white.

"I know that the world seems bent on stopping you."

He places his hands back on the table.

97

"But you can do it. You can do it. And nothing will be the same if you don't just keep going. Please keep going."

"I will, I'll keep going."

Nigel bursts from the chair and picks up the roll of wallpaper. Jess notices the tears brimming in his eyes.

"Please keep going."

"I'll keep going. I promise."

He hoists the wallpaper to his shoulder.

"Would you like to stay longer?" she asks.

He leans forward to peer out at the sky.

"This window is closing I think."

"What do you mean?"

"It's time for me to get up there and make one big attempt."

"I'm really not following you."

"Have you been to Kenneth Bluff?"

"Of course, several times."

"At sunrise?"

"No, not at sunrise."

"If it's going to happen at all, it's going to happen there."

He turns towards the door.

"Wait, what's going to happen? What are you doing up there?"

He pauses at the door.

"Remember the pieces, the scattering of infinitesimally small fragments? Well I think I have one more chance. I'm putting everything in one place. Maybe I can make them stay."

Jess rises from her chair and follows him to the door.

"I didn't get your name."

Nigel walks out onto the sidewalk, pointing the wallpaper towards the hills.

"How about I tell you my name next time."

"What? Next time?"

She watches him walk down 7th street all the way until he's barely visible between the trees lining the sidewalk, when he turns the corner.

Jess returns to her seat. She swirls the coffee in her mug.

well that was different

The espresso machine whirs quietly behind her.

that cut is no good, looks like he wiped the blood off once and just left it there

She watches the light reflect off the coffee, a soft white rectangular stain spreading over its smooth surface.

the thing about projects is how hard it is to just finish them

She leans her head against the window. She watches the dark clouds spread farther away from the hills.

how hard it is, when you've had your mind set on it for so long, when it consumes you, how hard it is to just finish it

She watches the clouds move slowly overhead for another moment, before downing the last of her coffee and pushing open the front door into the late afternoon.

As the steam begins sputtering out of the kettle and rising to the ceiling, Mandy retrieves the mugs from the cupboard and arranges them on the counter.

In the living room, Lapis runs her finger over the little succulent plant on the coffee table. Randell stands in the center of the room, his hands in the pockets of his jacket.

"I told you, he doesn't have a cell phone. University email account, that's it"

"Well are there any other buildings on campus where he might have gone to study?"

"Not that I know of, and he wouldn't have time. I'm telling you he's always there."

"And you're sure there's no way he's at the library now?"

"I told you I looked; I went down every aisle. Probably scared some people running around that place."

He plants his feet firmly against the ground, holding his space.

"But that's not the main point. I knew he wouldn't be there. He said he was coming back earlier than usual. I think he got attacked on his way home, that's what I think."

"But if he left you that note that means he made it home."

"Right, but he's a different kind of guy. He doesn't always think about the things... he doesn't always seem the most...logical you could say. But he's smart, I'll tell you that."

Mandy pours the tea carefully into each mug.

"His note said he's going to go 'fix things' right? If he was assaulted on his way home, do you think he could be trying to get back at the person somehow?"

"No way, not him. I don't know what fixing it means to him, but I can guarantee you it doesn't involve violence."

Mandy carries the mugs into the living room, setting them down carefully on the coffee table.

"I made you some just in case, Randell," Mandy says as she arranges the mugs on wooden coasters.

"Oh, I appreciate that."

"I was wondering," Mandy continues as she settles into the couch next to Lapis, "how long you've been roommates with him. Were you friends before?"

Randell doesn't respond immediately. He shuffles his feet and glances up at Lapis before turning back to Mandy. Lapis sits quietly, running her fingers slowly over the succulent.

"I haven't known him long, just for a few months. When I, uh, when I came here this summer, I didn't have anywhere to go. Maybe you know some about the, uh...the past."

100

He scratches the back of his head. Lapis smiles weakly at the floor, her eyes distant.

"Not really, and I don't mean to pry. I was just trying to get a better sense of who Nigel is."

Randell clears his throat.

"Well, I uh I left the little town where Lapis and I went to high school. It's not too far away, about 15 miles west on the highway. Came here with not much. Some clothes and a backpack. I didn't have anywhere to stay so I slept in the park downtown. It was summer, and there were lots of folks hanging out down there."

Lapis brings her eyes to focus on Randell, holding them there.

"And it was just a random day, I was sitting on a bench roasting out there in the sun, all the shady spots were taken, just sitting there frying, and this guy just walks up and talks to me. Sat down on the bench with me and just talked. I knew he was a little different right away, but we just talked about all kinds of things. A bunch of different things all at once. Then he asked if I had anywhere to stay. Here's the thing I looked rough, okay? Sun-burnt, scraggly, hadn't showered in two weeks... I said 'No, I don't.' And he just asked if I'd like to move in with him."

"That was really kind of him," Lapis says softly.

when he left town in the summer

"Sure was. He's on some big scholarship so he said don't sweat the rent, but I said no way am I mooching off this guy. So he helped me get a job at the little store on the corner there. That's just the kind of guy he is. You never know what he's gonna do or say next, but he just loves people. If he did get attacked, he's not seeking revenge, I'll promise you that."

Randell scratches the back of his head. Lapis picks up a mug from the table, holding it in both hands, watching the steam rise slowly.

left town in the summer and never came to say good-bye

101

Mandy tries to think of something to say.

"So he told you he would be back earlier than usual, was there something else he had planned to do last night?"

"Yeah, he's on this whole interior design kick right now. I don't know, he might have been getting something for that. But you gotta understand, leaving early for him is still pretty late. I got home from work just after midnight, and he wasn't there. I figured he changed his mind or got caught up with one of his papers or something."

Lapis watches the steam rise from the mug.

came in from the orchard that day and susan couldn't wait to tell me that she got off the phone with someone and they finally ran him out, he's gone, isn't that good news?

"Here's the part that's confusing," Mandy chimes in. "Why would he come back to write that note just to leave again? And the note doesn't leave a clear impression of where he went. Wouldn't he want to let you know where he was going instead of just disappearing?"

"Like I say, he's a different kind of guy. I'm sure in his mind he made it perfectly obvious where he would be going and what he's doing. Or I guess the other possibility is he just doesn't get why disappearing would concern me. But with his personality...he belongs in classrooms, libraries, that's where he belongs, not everyone can make it out there on the streets."

Lapis stares at the bottom of the mug.

running out into the orchard alone, susan calling after me, running out there alone in the peach trees where I took him that first time, deep in the grove

"Maybe he went to stay somewhere else? With a friend?"

"I guess it's possible. I just don't know who that would be. For how eager he is to meet strangers, I don't think he has many close friends."

He shuffles his boots against the floor. It's silent.

102

and now he's hovering there across the room dark ghost

"Lapis, can I ask you something?"

Lapis breaks out of her trance.

"Yeah?"

"I'm just confused, how are you a student here?"

"I'm a student here," she says quickly. "I'm really enjoying it. Maybe we should look at his note again."

"What? I just don't get how. Don't you have to…"

"Let's stay focused on finding Nigel right now."

"I'm just asking, did you do an online program to finish high school?"

"Well, I just…"

She turns to Mandy, then back to Randell.

"No, I didn't do any program to finish high school. I never went back after everything."

"Then how are you going to college here?"

"I just go to classes. Usually just big lecture hall classes when the professor doesn't know anyone. But I also wanted to go to some smaller classes, which was more complicated."

She looks again at the bottom of the mug.

"Hey uhm, sorry, I didn't mean to unravel your story there."

The room is silent for a few moments.

"Mandy," Randell says to break the silence, "could you point me towards your restroom?"

"It's to the left at the end of the hall."

The wood floors creak as Randell crosses the room and disappears into the hallway. From the living room, Lapis and Mandy hear the bathroom door shut. They sit on the couch silently. Mandy tries to think of something to say.

"I'm sorry I lied about being a student," Lapis says, staring into her mug.

"You don't have to be sorry, you had me fooled."

"But it wasn't about deceiving anyone. I just wanted to meet some new people, some new friends. I wasn't trying to trick anyone. I'm just really sorry."

"Hey. It's okay, I get why you did it. And I'm glad you did it, because I wouldn't have met you otherwise."

Lapis looks up from her mug and turns to Mandy.

"Thanks for saying that. I'm really glad I got to meet you too."

Randell zips his black jeans and flushes the toilet.

Mandy notices the trembling in Lapis' hands as she sets the mug on the table.

"Is everything okay? Do you need anything?"

"I'm sorry I couldn't show you that garden today."

"That's okay, it's really kind of you to help him with this."

"It's just hard. I didn't expect...I really wasn't prepared to see him."

Randell leans against the counter and stares into his own eyes.

"Did you know he was living here in town?"

"No, I had no idea where he was."

crying under the peach trees

"You're doing a really brave thing, Lapis."

"You think so?"

They meet each other's eyes.

"I know so."

"I just don't know if it's any help. And getting tossed into this all of a sudden, right when I was moving on. And I feel bad about bringing you into it."

"Don't feel bad about that. I'm here for you. I want to help you through it."

Randell stares into the streaks of red in his eyes.

tell her you just can't stay, tell her your sorry about this and maybe we can talk about it later. Jesus fuck what a shit show

104

"After this, I promise I'll take you to that garden. And to other places, we can go anywhere."

"Have you ever been to Kenneth bluff?"

"No, see that's what I want to do. We should go to all those places. And bring Jess too!"

"I don't know if she would want to come."

Jess crosses the street into the old neighborhood.

that's the thing with projects he said. is finishing them

"Well that's okay. Hiking isn't for everyone. And there's so many other adventures out there, so many avenues of experience. And we can explore all of them."

"Well we have your show tomorrow, right?"

"I guess that's already coming up tomorrow. Would Jess have a good time at something like that."

"I'm not sure, she said she might be able to come."

Randell closes his eyes and tries to stay calm.

just say you have to go and leave it at that. no need to rehash everything. don't go into all that it's just not the place. say thank you for your help but you're leaving now

"I don't mean to overstep anything," Lapis says cautiously, "but is everything okay with you and her? I'm just getting the sense that there's some tension."

"Things could be better."

"Every relationship has its ups and downs; I hope those things get better soon."

"We'll see."

Mandy turns to face Lapis again.

but I get it now. that night was supposed to be the end, it was supposed to be all over, I was supposed to walk out the door

"You're right, there's always ups and downs."

but don't say that just tell her you have to tell her just do it

"Maybe when she gets through this situation with that class things will get better."

105

just say it just say it now i can't live here anymore i can't be with her anymore

"Yeah, you're probably right."

and i want to hike to kenneth bluff and watch the sunrise and hold you

"It's always hard this time of year when the days get so short."

Randell rubs his hands over his eyes.

just don't say anything stupid please just for once don't fuck everything up

"Maybe you two could use a fun night together. A night to just let loose. Some music and dancing might be just what she needs to destress from everything going on."

"I think you're right."

no you're wrong you're wrong you're wrong

Jess walks down the sidewalk, watching the clouds.

"And afterwards we can all hang out and maybe watch a movie or something."

"I'm excited to hear you play."

"I'm a little nervous, I haven't performed in a long time."

"I know you'll be great."

They're silent for a moment.

just try to say something just try say that you need to talk

"Can I tell you something?"

"Yeah, of course, anything."

"I just...I don't know how."

just say it just let it out

"Just say it in the way that comes easiest, that's the best way."

"I...uhm..."

She hears footsteps on the concrete walkway outside.

"Oh...I..."

"What is it, Mandy?"

106

"I think Jess is here."

She watches the knob twist and the door swing wide, she meets Jess' eyes as soon as she appears in the doorway.

"Jess. You're home. How was your day?"

Jess stands in the doorway for a moment before stepping into the living room. She opens her mouth but doesn't say anything.

no. no way. she couldn't

Lapis smiles up at Jess from the couch.

"I'm Lapis, Mandy's friend from class. It's nice to finally meet you."

"Hi. It's nice to meet you too."

she couldn't. no way. she couldn't do that to me

"We got caught up in a situation before our class started and it's kind of taking over our afternoon."

Jess steps through the living room and sets her bag down near her desk.

"Oh. A situation. That's interesting. Is that why you ignored me all day?"

Mandy turns her eyes towards the floor.

she wants to do this in front of her, right in front of her

"I didn't mean to ignore you; we were just trying to help somebody."

Lapis watches Jess closely.

"Good for them. Well I have a lot of work to do tonight, so maybe…"

Jess trails off when she hears footsteps in the hallway.

"Who is that?"

Randell appears in the hallway, filling up the door frame as he passes through it.

"Oh, hey. You must be the roommate. I'm Randell."

"Uhm."

107

"Thank you for letting us use your living room as a kind of strategy center. It's been a big help. Unfortunately, I'm going to have to be going now."

Jess shoots a glance at Mandy.

"This is our friend Randell," Mandy says. "We've been trying to help him find his roommate who has been missing."

"But now I've got to get back to actually looking for him. Runnin outta daylight."

Randell starts towards the door.

"What's going on here?" Jess asks, standing up out of her chair. "Mandy, tell me what's going on here."

Lapis rises from the couch and takes a step towards the center of the room.

"Randell's roommate has gone missing. We came here to think and try to get a better idea of how we should proceed."

"So that's why you two were cuddled up together on the couch, but what were you doing back there?"

"Just using the restroom before I shove off is all. And now I'm off."

Randell makes another attempt towards the door.

"No wait a second," Jess says. "I want you to tell me what those two were up to."

"What?"

"Those two."

"Shit, I don't know. I understand Mandy there is your...girlfriend I guess. And Lapis there, well she's friends with her. I'm not sure what else you're looking for."

"Friends cuddling on the couch when you think I won't be back. That's the story?"

Lapis narrows her eyes. Mandy stares at the floor *please stop*.

"Well, hey let's just wait just a second here. Pump the brakes. You're accusing your girlfriend of messin around with

108

Lapis? I don't mean to be dismissive, but you're barkin up the wrong tree there."

"And what are you looking at?" Jess asks when she notices Lapis' eyes.

"I don't think you're being very kind to your partner right now," Lapis says firmly.

"Oh you don't?"

"No. I think you're overstepping boundaries, making accusations, and just generally being kind of an ass."

"Boundaries. That's funny. You're telling me about boundaries."

"We're friends. She invited Randell and me over here to help him with something and you're acting like she's done something wrong. What has she done wrong?"

"This is where you leave. Now you're overstepping your boundaries."

"If I'm overstepping a boundary I apologize. I just don't think you're making your partner feel very safe."

Mandy watches the cracks between the floorboards run towards the wall *please everyone stops.*

"All right, ladies, let's simmer down."

"You need to shut the fuck up," Jess responds.

"Okay, it's time for me to leave."

"No, Randell, not yet," Lapis says.

Randell feels his back brush the wall. He tries to calm the pain.

"You both need to get the fuck out of my house so Mandy and I can resolve this."

"That's not happening until I think she's safe."

The cracks across the floor to the wall silently, nearly invisible *please.*

"What do you think you're doing? You're not helping anything."

109

"If we can settle down we can maybe move on with what we were doing."

"Don't tell me to settle down!" Jess says loudly.

Mandy watches the cracks recede away from her as she rises from the couch. She hears a voice emerging from inside her, pouring out.

"It's okay Jess. Let's take a step back before things escalate."

She doesn't recognize the voice. It's clear and strong, rising out of her in smooth, steady waves.

"We think someone's in real danger tonight. He's vulnerable, alone, and possibly hurt. We need to put these issues on the back burner for the time being until we can devise a plan for how we're going to help get him out of danger."

The voice feels unfamiliar in her throat, but every time she opens her mouth, she feels it surging out of her again.

"If you'd like, we could find another place to make our plan. But I would rather we stay here."

Jess stands silently in the center of the room. Randell presses his back against the wall. Lapis watches Mandy in quiet awe.

"Okay," Jess says after a long pause. "Okay, what's the situation? Maybe I can help."

"That would be amazing," Mandy says. "Do you want to describe the situation again, Randell?"

"You probably know it better than I do at this point," he replies.

"Well Randell was expecting his roommate would be back at their apartment from the library at some point yesterday evening. Randell got home from work around midnight and Nigel wasn't there. He didn't think anything of it because apparently Nigel is known for extended study sessions at the library. The next morning, Nigel still hadn't shown up at the apartment. But Randell found a note from Nigel saying that he

110

had met some kind of negative encounter with someone late at night and he has to fix it somehow. His words."

"Is he trying to get back at the person?" Jess asks.

"Randell doesn't believe that to be a possibility. He says that Nigel has an eccentric personality and sometimes responds to situations in unconventional ways."

"So that's where we stand?"

"That's where we stand."

Jess spends a moment in thought.

"I assume he hasn't been answering his phone."

"He doesn't have one," Randell says from his position against the wall.

"What was he studying last night?" Lapis asks.

"I don't see how that's relevant," Jess says.

"I'm just wondering."

"He's real into poetry and all that. What book did he say? I think he said the book was called Keats."

"Keats?"

"Yeah, that's what it was."

"Keats is the name of a poet, Randell."

"Well shit if I know. That's just what he said."

"That's interesting. We're reading Keats in our class right now."

"He reads non-stop. That's his thing."

"Is there anywhere else he could have gone last night? Grocery store?"

"I was telling them, he's been on this interior design kick, changing up the kitchen a bunch, moving things around. I guess it's possible. That's one of the reasons I was sure he would be back earlier than usual. He was planning on putting up some new wallpaper in the kitchen."

Jess looks up from the floor.

"You said wallpaper?"

Mandy and Lapis notice the change in her voice.

111

"Yeah. He was worried it didn't give him the right feeling I guess. I don't know. It's getting dark. It might be time for me to head out and do some looking."

"Wait," Jess says. Her eyes are wide. She glances around the room.

"Wait," she says again. "I think...okay, I just met some literally within the last hour. At Presto. He was really excited about talking to someone. But he had with him a big roll of blue wallpaper."

"You're kidding."

"He had a roll of blue wallpaper. He was ordering at the counter and it kind of fell near where I was sitting, and he came to pick it up and we started talking somehow. But I never got his name."

"What did he look like?"

"Kind of short. He looked like he might have spent the night outside, talking about a lot of different things really fast."

"That's him. No question. Where was it?"

"Just wait a second Randell, don't rush off yet." Mandy says.

"That's him, a million percent that's him."

"You had a conversation with him but didn't get his name?"

"It was weird. It wasn't a normal conversation. I mean he asked questions and got really enthusiastic about my activist stuff. I asked his name and…"

"And what?" Randell asks.

"He said something really vague and strange."

"That also sounds like him. What was it?"

"I asked his name and he said, 'I'll tell you next time.'"

"That's a little creepy," Lapis says.

"But it wasn't. He was so innocent, so excited and innocent. But the other thing. Oh wow, okay."

112

"What? What is it?" Randell seems ready to burst through the ceiling and out into the night.

"He was hurt. He had this bad cut on his eye, around his eye. I tried to ask him about it, but he just deflected and started talking about a bunch of other things."

"Jesus Christ. Okay. I'm outta here. I'm gonna go find him."

"No wait, I…"

"I'm glad you saw him. That's a crazy coincidence. I know where the Presto cafe is, he can't have gone far."

"But he won't be there, just listen."

"Sure he won't, but he'll be in the area."

"Just up and listen for a second."

"Stop, Randell," Lapis says to him.

Randell stops at the door.

"Okay, what?"

"He won't be in the area, but I think I know where he's going. He was talking, the main thing we talked about was projects, he kept coming back to it. His project, my project. And he was saying his project is in danger of failing and he has one more chance to fix it or finish it."

"That sounds like what he said in the note," Mandy says.

"Okay. But what does that tell us?"

"I think... he was kind of vague about this, but he asked about Kenneth Bluff, that cliff outside of town. He said that maybe he could finish his project there."

"That's miles away. That's where he said he's going?"

"That's what it sounded like."

"Well there's no way he's there yet if he's on foot."

"When did you say you saw him, an hour ago?"

"Probably over an hour ago now."

"Jess did he say what he was going to do there?" Mandy asks.

"He said he could finish his project there."

113

"Jesus. Okay."

"Can we borrow your car Jess?"

"I'll drive. Come on. Is everybody dressed warm enough? It's a hike."

They file out of the house quickly and cross the lawn to Jess' car on the street.

"I'll take shotgun so I can watch the road for him," Randell says.

Jess unlocks the car. Mandy and Lapis take their seats in the back.

"Get on the highway going west," Randell tells Jess.

"I know where it is. I've been there."

Jess pulls into the road and drives down the street. The group is silent for a few moments. Jess takes a left turn at a stop light and heads towards the highway.

"He's gonna be out on that highway somewhere if he meant to go to Kenneth bluff. Out on that highway…"

Randell stares out the window. In the back seat, Lapis closes her eyes and breathes.

this highway

Jess accelerates as they climb onto the highway on-ramp. As the ramp joins the highway heading west, Jess watches the last trace of light linger over the dark western hills.

"Somewhere out here, he'll be walking along the narrow shoulder, crazy bastard."

out here driving fast that night

Lapis breathes. Mandy turns her head slightly to her. Jess accelerates onto the highway. The last band of light receding under the hills.

"He made it out here a ways, I'll give him that, always in a hurry."

Jess hears the quiet tremble in his voice, the slow-rising fear.

114

"I think we're more likely going to be hiking up the trail before we find him," she says.

"Narrow shoulder, no room to walk."

out here on the road screaming at each other

"There's no guarantee he walked all the way out here," Mandy says. "He could have gotten a ride. That's probably more likely."

Lapis keeps her eyes closed.

just so angry at me

"Any second now he'll be coming up on the road."

then next thing BOOM

Mandy notices the tension in Lapis' shoulders.

"She's right. He probably got a ride out here," Jess says. "Any minute now."

Jess glances over at Randell, sees him staring forward at the road, his eyes blank.

Lapis draws a deep inhale.

and i told him over and over again it's not that you were wrong for intervening... i just saw something in your eyes, something terrible, something i never wanted to see again

She opens her eyes.

but i couldn't erase it from my memory, and when i looked at you it was all i saw, that dark something, that anger, rage...

Mandy watches the road from the backseat. She hears Lapis breathing softly next to her.

"Almost to the lake. Trailhead's just a ways after that."

"I know. I've been here before."

Mandy watches the yellow lines on the road disappear underneath the car.

that was in the summer just out of high school and we drove down here to visit and look around...and i looked at her the whole drive, windows down, warm sun

Lapis leans her head forward slightly to see Randell's face in the mirror.

and i knew that wasn't you, but you were gone, i knew you were gone

She sees his eyes staring blankly forward at the road.

and she told me she needed some time to process things. bullshit. i scared her is what i did. i scared her when i beat the piss outta that kid. cause i took action that's what i did. i saw what was wrong and i stopped it

She watches his eyes through the darkness of the backseat, sees them cutting through the long shadows, settling blankly on the mirror.

and he was just gone, after the trees by the lake, deep in the grove, he was just gone

"Be careful up here," Randell says.

no don't do this

"I'll be careful."

"People go fast through here. Keep an eye out"

no knock this off right now don't do this keep it together

"I will, Randell."

just stop and shut up or you'll really hurt her, no need to bring that shit up

He takes a short glance into the rear-view mirror. Lapis darts her eyes away.

don't say anything, remember what this is about

Jess keeps both hands on the wheel.

but it's been a couple years now since I took Mandy out here. just after high school. walked around campus, looking at all the buildings, all the trees

She watches the road unfold before her under the headlights.

couldn't wait to start, it's funny...how excited i was... to dive in....to start

Randell watches the road.

116

here it comes

The lake appears beside the highway, a massive dark mass, sprawling endlessly into the night.

there she is, been a while

Lapis watches the lake emerge from between the trees.

impenetrable darkness, there she is, dark and still and... dreaming

"There's the lake," Randell says. "Trailhead's just another mile or so."

where are you buddy... are you out there... are you okay

"Where's the lake?" Mandy asks.

"Just off to our right here, you can't see it?"

"You've been here before, Mandy, remember?"

"But it just looks like darkness out there."

"It's out there."

"It's a new moon tonight," Lapis says. "So there's no moonlight reflecting off of it. But you should see it when the moon's really glowing. It's like nothing you've ever seen before. Those full moon nights."

Mandy looks out the window at the darkness.

back when things were easy with us we came here

"New moon. It's a good thing we brought the flashlight," she says.

"Here it is, right up here," Randell says suddenly.

Jess slows down and turns off into a gravel enclave on the shore of the lake. The enclave is a small circle of gravel cut into the trees, situated between the highway and the edge of the lake.

"Well, here we are," Jess says as she draws the keys from the ignition. The group exits the car and walks towards the trailhead, a small break in the trees where the gravel extends into the forest.

"If we're going to do this we better get started," Jess says. "It's not exactly a short hike."

117

"It's only just over a mile to the bluff," Randell says.

"But the incline will make that mile feel like ten," Mandy says. "We better start walking. Do you have that flashlight, Jess?"

Jess clicks the flashlight on and shines it into the trees. The light illuminates the trail into the forest.

"Let's stay close together. The trail gets narrow. Jess, you can go first with the light."

When the gravel path gives way to the narrow dirt trail the group falls into single file. Jess keeps the light forward, illuminating the rocks and twisted roots rising out of the trail.

"Watch your step," Jess says.

Lapis follows closely after her, stepping easily over the roots, watching the light in the ferns and undergrowth.

strange being out here now, finding everything again as if I never left

Jess tries to glance around Lapis' shoulder to get a look at Mandy.

but something's gotten into her, something's different

Randell feels a pulsing in his back as the trail begins to steepen.

where are you man... are you in these woods... are you. Jesus

He holds his back with both hands as they climb higher.

"It gets steeper now for a while," Mandy says over her shoulder.

Jess watches the light pouring forward from Mandy's hand from behind Lapis. Mandy points the light up the trail, illuminating the steep incline.

something i've never seen from her, even her voice sounds different

The trees grow taller as they climb higher. Mandy directs the light squarely down the middle of the trail, shining

118

just slightly on the broad trunks of the massive trees lining the trail.

Lapis takes big, slow steps, watching the ferns wavering slowly beside them.

and being out here in the middle of all this, out on that road, now being up here, it's so surreal

Randell watches Jess recede away from him. His legs feel heavy. Each step sends a surge of hot pain through his back. He looks up to find Mandy's light glowing farther away than before, up higher on the trail, shining through the ferns.

Jesus man why are you doing this to me? why'd you have to run off and hide like this, what's that do, what are you fixing by this

He steps over a rock and feels his back tighten suddenly.

"Shit," he says through gritted teeth as he drops to one knee.

Jess hears him and turns around.

"Hey, hold up! Randell is down."

She walks back down the trail and squats down.

"Are you okay?"

"Yeah. Doing great," he says trying to rise to his feet.

"Stay down, just wait a second."

"Are you okay? What's wrong?" Lapis asks, kneeling beside him.

"I'm okay, just got a little pinch in my back is all...uh Mandy can you point that thing somewhere else, please? Just fine. I can get up."

"Are you sure? Are you injured?"

"I wouldn't say injured. Just a little sore is all. I can make it up there."

"Randell, just wait. Take a minute and rest. You don't need to be a hero right now."

"Well, he's out here somewhere and it's dark and he's alone. So, let's get going."

119

He gets to his feet with great exertion.

"Randell," Lapis says gently. "It's okay, sit back down."

"I'm okay, Jesus, let's get going now. Come on."

"Randell, you're bent over. How much pain are you in?"

"It's nothing."

"It's okay to feel pain. It's okay. I know you're tough, but you're hurt right now and need to sit down."

Randell hesitates. He looks up at the trees.

"Jesus."

He settles onto his knee, then slowly lowers himself all the way to the ground.

"Well, shit," he says. "I guess I owe all of you an apology. I got you all the way out here and now I can't make it to the top. I guess we'll have to call somebody or something."

"Maybe not," Mandy says. "Lapis, do you think you can make the hike and see if he's up there? I don't want you to go alone, of course. Jess, maybe you could stay…"

"I'll go with her." Jess says as she rises from her squat. "We'll go up there and check it out."

"Okay, that works. And I'll stay here with Randell."

"Hey, that's okay. I appreciate it. But you really don't have to."

"You shouldn't be out here alone," Mandy says. "I'll stay."

She turns to Lapis and hands her the flashlight.

"Do either of you have service up here?"

Jess and Lapis both draw their phones from their pocket to check.

"I don't," Jess says.

"Me either, but sometimes you can get some from the top."

"Well, if you find him up there, try to call me."

"We better get going," Jess says.

120

Lapis points the light back up the trail. They're still for a moment, watching the light spread out over the trees.

"Be safe," Mandy calls as they turn up the trail.

Randell watches their dark silhouettes climb farther away, the light growing smaller.

funny the way things go...sure are funny the way things go

The light dances through the boughs of the Douglas Firs.

for her to be here now...walking up there...for her to be here now... sure is strange the way things go

"Are you alright, Randell?" Mandy asks as she takes a seat on the trail beside him.

"I know this has been a really stressful day."

"Yeah, I'm doing alright. I can't tell you how much I appreciate you all coming out here to look for him. Even if he's not up there...I can't tell you...for someone you don't even know."

"Helping people, whatever the circumstances, shouldn't be a question," she says.

"Man, that's the truth. It's sad to see how people just ignore things...when something's obviously going wrong. I think you're right. Still, I can't tell you how much..."

He trails off as he gazes off into the dark woods.

"So how long have you been friends with Lapis?"

"Oh. Well, not too long, only a few days. We just met earlier this week in a class."

"Only a few days, huh."

He turns to look up the trail.

"Looks like they made it around the bend. Not too much farther to the bluff after that."

They sit in silence for a moment, listening to the breeze rustling the trees softly.

"Hopefully, it doesn't rain on us," she says.

"It won't."

They're silent for another moment.

"So," Mandy begins, "how long were you and Lapis together?"

"Couple years, I guess. Most of high school. But we had to hide it for most of that time."

"Why was that?"

"It's kind of a backwards town. We're not too far away, it's just a little farther down the highway. And the school, it was just kind of a shit show. She got in trouble for weed and stuff. And I kind of had this image...athlete, football, that kind of thing. So, we would sneak out to different places like this and hangout. Then she moved in with these Christians who have an orchard outside of town. So, then we really had to be careful. I'm jabberin' on I guess."

"No, go on, I'm interested."

"Well, senior year we said fuck it we're not gonna hide it anymore. The Christian family she was staying with actually thought it was a good idea, ya know because I had this image, football image. So, we were public that year. Then things just kind of fell apart at the end of the year. As things go."

They're silent again. Mandy stares into the darkness between the trees.

"But it seems it like she's finding a place for herself here, right? Over in the city I mean, around university type people."

"Yeah. You know I was just as surprised as you when I found out she's not technically enrolled at the university. She's one of the smartest people I've met."

"Yeah, she's real bright."

He scratches the ground with his finger.

"So, how long have you and Jess been together?"

"It's been a couple years now. Senior year of high school."

"Man. And you both wanted to go to college here?"

122

"Well, it was Jess at first. I kind of followed along. But I'm glad I did. It's been great."

The hole under Randell's finger grows deeper.

"I don't mean to pry, overstep or anything. But it seemed like things got a little heated back at the house. Like there was some kind of jealousy or something like that."

"Things are a little rough right now, a little tense. I think Jess thought something was going on with Lapis. It was just a misunderstanding."

"Again, I don't mean to cross any line. And I know I was in the bathroom. But it just seemed like things escalated a little quickly. Like she was pretty quick to assume that you were doing something wrong. Which, well, I don't know."

"She's under a lot of stress. But you're right. Lapis was right. It wasn't good. Wasn't good at all. And something has to change."

"No easy thing," Randell says, "change."

"I was a little surprised Jess volunteered to go up there with Lapis, after what happened at the house," she says.

"Yeah. Who knows? Maybe she got over it, cooled her jets a little."

"Yeah, maybe."

but that's not it. that's not her. she didn't want to go up there with Lapis, but she really didn't want me going up there with Lapis. she just wanted to keep us separate

"Who knows. Funny the way things go. Sure funny. And strange... the way things go."

Up the trail Lapis holds the flashlight, illuminating the path forward.

"Shouldn't be much farther now, right?"

"It's still a ways," Lapis replies.

"I remember getting around that bend and being almost to the top."

"Maybe the darkness makes it seem like we're going faster than we are. Because we have less visual aid to gage our relative progress."

"Maybe. It just feels like we should have been there already."

Lapis doesn't respond.

"Hold that flashlight steady, don't let it waver so much. I can't see the trail."

well maybe if you would have stayed down there with Randell like Mandy asked you to. but you couldn't stand for her to be alone with me.

Jess watches the trail, taking each step deliberately.

bullshit

Lapis steadies her eyes on the faintest point of the light's reach.

that's just so possessive, controlling, unfair. what Mandy's not allowed to have friends?

Jess steps over the thick roots protruding from under the trail.

but it's the right thing. being out here. even if I have lots of work to do, even if everything's falling apart. this is the right thing

The trail widens as it reaches the top of the incline, wide enough for two people to walk side by side.

Jess steps forward to Lapis' side. They're silent for a few moments.

this is the right thing. I know it is. Even if it's confusing, even if everything's falling apart

"Lapis?"

"Yeah?"

Lapis keeps her eyes forward, fixed on the place where the light dissolves into the trees.

"I'm sorry about what happened back at our house. It was wrong of me to come in and assume there was something

124

going on with you and Mandy. And you were right to call me out about it."

"I don't think you have to apologize to me."

"What? Why?"

"I mean, I appreciate it. But I think Mandy is the one you owe an apology to."

"Yeah. You're right. You're totally right. I just came in with all my emotional baggage from the day and everything that's been going on."

"It happens," Lapis says.

Mandy tilts her head backwards and stares at the sky, a blank jagged circle surrounded by the dark figures of the trees.

"It's wild how dark it gets out here."

"Sure is. I've forgotten I think."

"Forgotten how dark it gets?"

"Yeah. And quiet too."

"There's something about this silence," Mandy says. "Something a little different than the other silence."

"What's the other silence?"

"I mean the kind of silence when you're falling asleep. In our house if there's no cars driving by, it gets so quiet, it's unsettling. But this isn't the same silence."

"Huh. What's the difference?"

"The difference...at home, in bed, it feels like a flat, stale, silence. Dead silence. But out here...it's almost like the silence out here is alive in some way, that there's something pulsing underneath it, inside of it, a vibrancy. It feels like I'm being watched."

"Who's watching?"

"I don't know. Maybe it's the silence."

"Man. That sounds like something Nigel would say."

the lake out there just beyond the trees

They stare into the trees silently.

125

"Being watched by the silence," Randell says. "Yeah, Nigel would love that."

"It's hard to explain exactly what it feels like. But you know that feeling, like you're being watched?"

"Sure, yeah. But how can the silence watch you?"

"But the silence just means everything. Everything is watching you. It doesn't need to be a person."

"That's interesting."

looming out there somewhere in its own darkness, in its own time

"The silence is just the noise something makes when it's sitting perfectly still. It's still alive in there."

They sit silently for a few moments before Randell clears his throat again.

"You know the lake we passed on the way in, the one you couldn't see?"

"Yeah."

"It's right there in front of us."

"How far?"

"Maybe a hundred feet, then down a little slope. Less than a hundred probably."

waiting there in front of us, looming in its massive silence

"That's amazing. So, could we see it from here if it were light?"

"I think so. But I guess the better question, with what you said, is could the lake see us from there?"

"I bet the lake can see us just fine without any light."

A mile up the trail, Lapis stops and points the flashlight into the trees.

"Mandy said you have an instructor that's causing a lot of problems in one of your classes."

"You could say that. He's totally incompetent and doesn't know what he's talking. Actually, it's worse than that. I

126

think he knows what he's doing and is just deliberately trying to pass along damaging information."

"What's the damaging information?"

"That American culture is a just democracy and its politics are some kind of glimmering example of playing by the rules and going through the proper channels, waiting for progress that kind of thing. He constantly erases the violence that pervades everything. And the danger and risk involved in demonstrating against these oppressive structures. He just ignores it."

"That's very shitty. I'm sorry you're having that experience."

"At this point, the thing that's even more disappointing is how the people I've reached out to in the department just refuse to do anything about it. That's what I've been working on all week. They just aren't interested in addressing the problem. They just say, 'we're here for you, we're listening' all that, but nothing happens."

"So, is there anything we can do?"

"It's not looking good. They're having this review tomorrow morning which is all formality and posturing. He'll say the right things, and everything stays the same."

"But if you can make your case to those people at the review, maybe they'll listen."

"Closed to undergrads."

"That's ridiculous."

"So, I don't know what's going to happen."

They walk in silence for a few moments.

"When I first got here," Jess begins again, "I was so excited about being in the middle of these conversations and being part of systemic change. I thought that's what it was all about. I thought that's what everyone was doing. But they're not."

"They're just performative?"

"That's one word for it. They know if they keep going through all the motions, they can maintain some kind of weird status in this whole structure. It's all elitist, it's all about exclusion."

"I think your instructor needs to know that what he's doing is not okay."

"You and me both."

"Why don't you just go to that review tomorrow, just crash their party and speak out."

Jess doesn't respond. They walk silently.

she doesn't want to talk about it anymore

"You were right. we really should have been there by now," Lapis says.

"Your relative progress thing must really be kicking in."

Lapis points the flashlight through the trees, searching for familiar landmarks.

"Well, there's no way we missed it. The trail just leads right to it. Maybe we're walking slower than we think."

"He's up here, I know he is."

"Let's hope so."

Mandy stares out into the ferns.

"Randell, can I ask you something?"

"Yeah, of course."

"So, Lapis can't enroll in college because she didn't graduate high school. Is that right?"

"Yeah, that's right."

"Can you tell me why? She's such a smart person and seems so passionate about everything, including learning."

Randell turns his eyes up to the small window of sky in between the trees.

out on the highway screaming

"Well, she just quit school I guess is the short answer. Things got all messed up. It's hard to say."

"You don't have to. It's not really my place to ask."

128

"Things got all messed up."

YOURE A MONSTER YOU DIDNT CARE

"Really, you don't have to. I'm sorry I brought it up."

"It's hard to say…."

and i sat there and wondered if there really was something evil inside me, just looking for any excuse to destroy somebody, just to let it all out, any excuse, and when i saw those idiots throwing at those poor kids...that was all i needed

"The music was playing real quiet."

"What music? When?"

"In the car. One of her tapes. Woman wailing on the radio."

"Randell, I don't understand."

so i closed my eyes and prayed. i asked god to take this thing out of me. i said she's right there's something wrong with me and this is how i can fix it

"I prayed, and I could hear the music."

"Lapis' music?"

"Then I saw the light."

i prayed and said please take this away, take it out of me i don't want to be angry anymore

Mandy notices the violent trembling in his hands.

"Hey, it's okay Randell. You're okay."

then when i opened my eyes that light was right there huge, covering everything

"People drive too fast on that highway, they always have. Lapis had that little truck from the orchard haulin down the road."

"You and Lapis were in a car accident?"

"Right there," he says and points into the forest. "Right over there."

"Was anyone hurt?"

"Not too bad. Argument. Things got all messed up. Jacked my back up real good."

129

"And then you moved to the city just to get away?"

"And I guess Lapis came too. It's funny. I've thought about her so much these last few months. Wondered how she was doing back in town, orchard and all that. Turns out she was probably less than a mile away. And now she's a mile above us looking for my roommate. Funny how stuff goes."

"I think we're getting close," Lapis says breathlessly.

"We better be."

"Yeah, this feels right. It's right up here."

They speed up their pace.

"Seems like the trees are pretty sparse up here," Lapis says.

"Look!" Jess calls. "It's right ahead. Just up that last incline."

"Do you think there's a chance you two could become friends again?" Mandy asks.

"I don't know. After tonight I think it might be better if we go our separate ways again. Seems like she's finding a groove for herself. Friends like you. I think she'd do better without the past coming up to her out of the crowd. For a while at least."

now that everything's so played out, stretched things so far now, and all the old feelings don't make any sense

Mandy sits silently, listening.

does he know? can he see me?

Randell places his hands on his lower back.

"Does your back feel any better?"

maybe he knows and he's just playing. maybe he's known the whole time. maybe he sees me. no way, he can't

"It feels alright. I'm gonna have a hell of a time getting off this hill."

no way he knows

"We can help you get down."

"I'll be fine. I'll just have to sweat it out."

130

and he shouldn't know. maybe...

Randell tries to rock himself onto his side.

maybe she doesn't need to know. not right now. I'll wait and then when things calm down, I'll tell her

"I think that's for the best."

"What is?" Mandy starts from her thoughts with alarm.

"For me to step away for a while. She has you, right? She has new friends."

"I think maybe you should ask her what she wants."

"This has just been a wild day. And I'm worn out. It's gonna be somethin gettin back down that hill."

Jess sees the trail open up out of the trees. She shines the flashlight on the opening.

"There it is, we made it."

even in the dark I recognize it, the way the trees look, opening onto the cliff, I remember it. up here with Mandy hot evening in the summer

Lapis breaks into a run as they approach the end of the trail. The trees and shrubs form a broad gateway at the end of the trail, opening to the view of the dark sky. They pass under the trees and out onto the bluff, a wide rock platform stretching into the darkness.

"Well, is he here?" Jess asks. "Shine the flashlight around."

up here by ourselves, and the pink clouds sunk just above our heads in the warm air

Lapis shines the light over the bluff. She sees a small figure near the edge of the bluff.

"Is that him? There at the edge?"

"I don't know, it's too far away."

"I don't want to shine the light right over there if it's not him."

"Who else would be up here right now?"

"I don't know, let's just walk over there."

131

Lapis keeps the flashlight low, shining it on the ground before them. They cross the bluff quickly, stepping over cracks in the rock and small plants growing on its rough face. The bluff narrows near the ledge, a thin, rocky cliff jutting out into the sky.

we laid there on that edge for hours, watching the sun drop over the orange smoky hills, watched it fall, who was I? who even was that?

"Hey there, are you Nigel?" Lapis asks.

The figure remains still.

"Hello? Are you Nigel?"

Suddenly the figure bursts up to a standing position, stepping forward towards them. Lapis keeps the flashlight pointed towards the ground. The figure steps forward, his shoes falling under the light. Jess looks at him in the darkness, notices the cut around his eye.

"We met this afternoon; do you remember me? I'm Jess, this is Lapis. We just came up here to make sure you were okay."

Nigel doesn't respond. Jess looks at his cut through the shadows.

he's not looking at us, he sees us maybe, but he's not looking at us

"Are you alright?" Lapis asks. "Do you need anything?"

Nigel leans his head back towards the sky.

"It's good to see you again Jess," he says softly.

"It's good to see you too. Randell is worried about you. He's down near the trailhead and wants to see you."

Nigel brings his eyes forward again.

"You're here. And he's here."

"Our friend is down there with him. He hurt his back and couldn't make it up here."

"I-I don't know what happened."

"That's okay. We're just glad we found you. Do you feel like you can make it back trail?"

132

"I remember his face. But...and I remember you Jess. But I don't remember how I got up here."

"That's totally okay. Do you need to rest? Or do you think you can make it down the trail?"

"I... I think I need this."

He steps back to the ledge and squats down, bringing the roll of wallpaper from the ground to his shoulder in one movement.

"I'm sorry I caused this stress. I don't know what happened...after his face it's all a... fuzzy, weird blur."

"Whose face?"

"I don't know him."

"We better start making our way down the hill. We can talk on the way if you'd like."

"Okay. Okay, I can do that."

The group walks back towards the tree line. Before they turn into the trees, Nigel stops and glances over his shoulder at the cliff. He peers over the ledge, down the mountain, for just a moment before turning and starting down the trail.

Friday October 15th

Randell sees the light shining in the trees from his spot on the ground.

"Hey, there's the light, look. They're back."

He struggles to his knees, then tries to balance himself on one knee.

"Stay there for a little," Mandy says, rising to her feet. "Yeah, I see them. They're just coming around the bend up there."

"Is he with them?"

"It's hard to tell, I can't see them clearly yet."

Randell lifts one of his legs up, then leans his hand against a tree and gets to his feet.

"Okay, this isn't too bad. Just a little stiff. Can you see them?"

"I just see the light really."

"Think the light sees you?"

Mandy glances back at Randell for a moment.

"Funny. Maybe we should meet them in the middle. Do you think you can walk?"

"Yeah, I think I can loosen it up a little bit by walking."

He takes a few slow steps up the path.

"Yeah, I think it'll loosen up," he says through his teeth.

Mandy turns back up the trail, watches the light growing bigger from up the slope.

"Let's see. I can see the person holding the flashlight. That's Jess, I think. And another shape, and yes I think I see a third person!"

"Crazy bastard really came up here. Shit."

Mandy waves an arm overhead as the light approaches.

"You made it! How was your hike?"

"Long." Jess calls down from off the slope.

Randell tries to stretch his back out as the group gets closer.

"Nigel's doing pretty well," Lapis says when they reach Mandy and Randell. "He doesn't remember a lot from the past 24 hours. He remembers meeting Jess and a few other things but doesn't quite understand how or why he got to the bluff."

Randell approaches Nigel slowly.

"It's good to see ya, buddy. I was gettin pretty worried about you, thought maybe you ran off to visit your friend Keats or something."

He spreads his arms wide. Nigel hesitates for an instant, before stepping forward into Randell's embrace.

"I'm sorry for scaring you. All of you," he says.

"I'm just glad you're alright man. Do you know what happened to your eye?"

134

"It's all very mixed up," he says, taking a step back. "I was trying to sort it out on the way down the trail, but it hasn't quite come back to me."

"We better get started back down to the car," Jess says.

"Just take your time thinking," Randell says as they start down the hill. "There's plenty of time to think. Need me to carry that roll? Can't believe you carried that up there."

all the time you want man you can take as long as you need but good lord that cut is bad

"How was it up there?" Mandy asks.

"It was good. Felt longer than we expected," Lapis says.

Jess walks along silently.

and now in just a few hours I have to decide if I want to keep this whole thing up, if I can keep going

Nigel walks quietly, stepping softly on the trail.

his face, and the pain, stepping out, blinding lights. i remember he was angry and i said something and he...then i was on the ground and i saw the blood. confession, dreaming, rush of emotion, the revelation, the project

Nigel walks quietly, swimming in his thoughts.

rush of...the project, and out alone in the lights, walking alone, confession, dreaming, pulsing something running and listening then feeling it vibrating until

He tries to concentrate. He sees Randell ahead of him, walking stiffly.

something hurt and I couldn't see, just lights, and the lights...and vibrations loudly in my head, sprinting through a forest carrying the scroll, spinning lights everywhere, the nightingale just ahead...rupture, fracture, implosion

He watches the stiff motions of Randell's stride. He hears the people around him speaking.

and then the sky opened up in front of me and all I saw was the darkness swirling, high over the abyss, a humming opacity and I opened the scroll

135

"He's probably had a concussion. That's how people get,
I've seen it football all the time. Can't remember anything."

"Could the concussion be related to the cut on his eye?"

"Maybe ask him, rather than just talking about him."

*the scroll unfurled slowly, I glanced into the abyss and
asked. I asked it simply plainly I asked it only once. and then I
listened*

"Maybe he sustained some kind of head trauma that also
caused the cut, a hard hit to the head or something."

"Why don't you just ask him?"

"I think he's a little out of it, Lapis."

*I listened for a while before I heard it. It came from
inside me, slowly at first. I looked back over the edge, out at the
vast space underneath me, space receding forever,*

A vehicle's headlights blink in front of him. The doors
open.

*then it was louder, and louder, and it surged through me
and I sat down on the ledge and I felt it, I listened, and it rose
through my body*

"Here, hop in, Nigel, we're gonna go back to the
apartment,"

*it was like music pulsing in my chest and I stared over
the edge and listened, and it slowly began to fade.*

He hears the car's engine come to life.

*and I let it fade away, and I smiled deep into that
massive darkness, that abyssal floor, and turned back to the
scroll*

"Are you hungry, Nigel?"

and I wrote it down

"Let's just let him chill out."

"But he probably hasn't eaten anything in 24 hours."

"Sure, he'll probably eat something when we get back to
the apartment."

I rolled the scroll together and sat with my eyes closed

136

"Are you cold, Nigel?"

"I'm telling you, he's in his world, you might just leave him be."

and i noticed I couldn't feel the music anymore, that it was silent and empty inside of me. I was hollow. and i just sat there in my emptiness...attuning to my silence

He watches the shadows dance across the dashboard.

"Just in his world. That's what he needs, trust me, I know how he is. Just needs to have his thoughts and settle down, he'll be alright. Trust me, that's just how he is."

Jess turns carefully into the alley, easing the car gently over a pothole.

"Careful over these potholes," Randell says.

"There, just at the end there." Jess brings the car to a stop. Randell opens the door and hops out.

"Come on, Nigel, let's go inside. Here I'll take the wallpaper. There we go."

"Let us know how he's doing tomorrow," Mandy says.

"I want to thank you all again for your help. I was a little fired up this afternoon, I know I was a little difficult. But you all really went above and beyond. I sure appreciate you all."

Lapis turns to Mandy, then back to Randell.

maybe i should, maybe it's the right thing maybe

"Can I come inside with you two?" Lapis says suddenly. Mandy looks up from the floor in surprise.

"I just want to make sure he's okay before I go home. I live close by, just a block away."

"Well, sure. I mean, yeah."

"I'll see you tomorrow hopefully," Lapis says to Mandy as she unbuckles her seatbelt and slides out of her seat. "And you too, Jess. At the show. Tomorrow night. If you're free."

"Have a good night, Lapis," Mandy says.

137

"You too, thanks for all the help today."

Lapis turns to Randell and Nigel as the car pulls away.

"You don't need to do this, he's doing okay, I think. Just ready to be home."

"I just want to make sure he's okay. That is, if it's alright with you Nigel? If I come in for a little?"

Nigel looks down from the sky.

"Yes," he says. "We would love for you to come in."

"Well, if he says so, here let me get the door."

Randell digs through the pocket of his jeans.

"Just a second, let me get this key, where is that thing?"

Lapis turns to look at Nigel. His eyes are turned upwards again.

"Here she is," Randell says as he pulls the key from his pocket. He switches on the light as they enter the apartment.

"Welcome back, Nigel."

Nigel sets the wallpaper down in the kitchen.

"I'm glad."

"What are you glad about?"

"About being here. After what happened."

"Are you remembering more about is?"

"Yes. I'm remembering more."

"Here, have a seat. We got an old couch here, but it's comfy. Go ahead, have a seat."

Lapis takes a seat on the couch. Randell slides his back down the wall to the floor, placing a bag of frozen vegetables behind him.

Nigel stands near the window, his eyes fixed on the sky through the glass.

"Do you remember more about what happened last night?"

"Yeah. I do."

"Don't feel like you need to talk all about it tonight if you don't want to."

138

"I remember him."

"Who do you remember?"

"I met a sad man last night. Or something like that. He was terrified and angry, it was horrible. And I didn't know what to do."

"Did he give you that cut?" Randell asks sitting up straight against the wall.

"He must have. I remember he was yelling...and then I was on the ground, then I just walked around town all night. I could barely see, everything was lights, and I just walked around. Then I would stop and write on the scroll for a few hours, trying to fix everything. The man...I just couldn't figure it out."

"What's the scroll?" Lapis asks.

"What did he look like?" Randell asks, rising from the floor.

"Don't start that again. Settle down."

"The thing about him...what was so upsetting I think is what he said. Even if he hit me, gave me a concussion, whatever, that's not what hurt. It was what he was saying. And the thing…"

"What did he look like?" Randell asks again.

"Randell, you need to let him talk. Sit back down and breathe. Save your emotional energy."

Nigel stares out the window, holding his eyes on something far away.

"I think he's a professor, or some kind of teacher. That's what I remember. He was talking about...I'm sorry it's all still kind of running together."

"That's okay."

"I think he's an instructor of some kind. But he has these dark things inside him. What was coming out of him. I couldn't understand. This self-loathing and anger, hate."

"Well, if he's an employee of the university we should have no problem finding him, right? Can't we find pictures of faculty and all that and you can see who he is?"

"I have another question, Nigel, if that's okay."

Nigel turns away from the window and stands in the middle of the room.

"What do you mean when you say, 'fix it?' You said that in the note you left for Randell and I'm just not sure what you mean by it."

"I just...." Nigel wraps his arms around his shoulders and squeezes tightly.

"See, now you're upsetting him. I told you to lay off the questions for a while, just give him a chance to get his bearings."

"I didn't mean to upset you, Nigel," she says.

"I just...something's broken," he sputters, crouching to the floor. "Something deep down. There's something totally damaged in the whole system. Not just the social or material even, certainly not just the political. It's damaged all the way down, broken. Fractured is the word and damaged."

"And you wanted to fix it," she says, kneeling down beside him. Randell holds the bag of vegetables to his back.

"One last chance," he says, squeezing his knees to his chest. "It was my last chance to fix it. Because when he left me there, I saw it. Broken all the way through, like a hollowed-out tree, rotten to its core, split. For him to be there and think and talk like he did. He's the fruit of that rotten tree. And one touch and it crumbles on itself."

"How did you want to fix it?"

"I thought I could find a way to get back, find my way back and finish everything. Get through the brokenness and find something. And I did it, I found it. It just wasn't what I was expecting."

"Nigel," Randell says, pressing his bag between his back and the wall. "I'm not following you, buddy. I know that's a

140

common occurrence. But this time I'm really lost as to what you're getting at."

Lapis watches Nigel silently.

"What did you find? Can you tell me?"

"Just for an instant. For one second. Maybe it wasn't even a second, but just a slice of time, the thinnest possible slice, it flashed in front of me. Then you found me up there at Kenneth bluff."

"What was it?"

"I think it was music. That's what it felt like. But it was in my chest. It just rang through me and then it was gone."

Randell looks up from the floor at Lapis.

well geez she's beaming up brighter than she has all day. beaming up like she did under those trees in the summer

"Do you think you could hear it again?"

Nigel focuses his eyes on Lapis for the first time.

following the silence all the way, spreading out over that vast...

"I don't think I need to."

"Why is that?"

those trees in the summer, yeah that's how she smiled. and the peaches were warm baking in the sun all day, layin there watching the sky

"I think the point was that it's okay if it doesn't happen again. I'll have to show you…"

she would talk about her dreams, about moving to the city and playing guitar, singing. she would talk and her eyes would just glow like that, glowing brighter and brighter and we'd pick a peach from the tree and bite into it

"I'll have to show you the scroll," Nigel says again as he stands and walks to the kitchen. He returns a moment later with the roll of wallpaper.

"So that's the scroll you were talking about."

under the sky out there, the summer breeze

141

Nigel sets the wallpaper on the floor and places a lamp beside it. He pushes on the roll with both hands, unrolling several feet of paper.

"Oh. Wow."

Randell sits up to get a look at the paper.

well i'll be damned. look at that

"How long did it take for you to write all this?"

"I'm not sure how long," he says.

"This is incredible. You packed every square inch of this with words. It must be... wow that's just incredible. What is it though?"

"It's not what I expected, it's not what I thought would happen. But it's also everything I needed. And more importantly, it's everything it needs to be."

"Well, who would have thought you were luggin around a freakin encyclopedia with you that whole time. I just thought you brought it with you because you liked how it looked. I'll be damned."

"Can I read some of it?" Lapis asks.

"Go ahead," he says. "But just know I didn't fix anything. I didn't fix what was broken."

Lapis settles into a cross-legged position on the floor next to the paper. She begins to read slowly. Randell presses his back against the bag of vegetables.

just don't ask about it, just let it rest, don't ask about any of it

Jess twists the key into the lock and pushes the door open.

don't ask about it

Mandy follows her into the house and sets the flashlight on the kitchen counter. She takes a glass from the cupboard and fills it with water.

don't ask, don't say anything

142

She takes a seat at her computer and begins to rub her forehead. Mandy returns from the kitchen with the glass of water.

"How are you doing?" she asks, taking a seat next to her. Jess looks up from her hands.

"Fine. I'm just exhausted."

"Why don't you go to sleep? It's late."

"I can't. I have that meeting tomorrow morning."

"But if the meeting is in the morning, maybe you should try to get some rest."

"But there's so much to do," she says, opening her computer.

"Like what? What haven't you done? How many hours have you spent on this so far this week?"

"There's a lot to do."

"Listen to me," she says. "You know exactly what you're going to say. You know exactly what's wrong and what needs to be done. How many times have you thought about what you would say in this situation? How many?"

"I don't know."

"How many? Ten times? Twenty times?"

"I've thought about it a lot, okay? Just stop."

"What?"

"Where's all this coming from? Why are you suddenly so eager to help with all this?"

stop

"What are you talking about?"

"Why now? Why are you so interested in this all of a sudden? I couldn't get you to say one thing about this all week. Now you have all this advice. Why?"

"I just wanted to help. That's all, I thought I could help you. Isn't that what you want?"

"Of course, I do. But I've been waiting for a long time for you to show some kind of emotion about any of this, some

143

sign that you care about what I'm going through, and you just sit there. Do you see why I'm frustrated?"

"I... yeah. I do. I was just trying to say that getting some sleep would help you with your meeting tomorrow."

"And if you knew about how I operate you would know that I can't sleep before something like this. I have to work. I have to do things. I can't just flip a switch and go to sleep. And you should know that about me by now."

"Look, I'm sorry. I was just trying to help. That's all."

leave it there don't say it

Mandy walks back to the kitchen and washes her glass in the sink.

is that what she would say? is that what she would do?

She stares out the kitchen window at the streetlights.

i don't think so

Lapis leans in closer to the wallpaper.

and she's sitting right here in this little shack all because of him. good lord. and he wrote up and down that thing

She follows the slanting lines with her finger.

and just like that she's sitting here. after everything that happened, she's right here. reading something off the back of some wallpaper. just funny. just funny how it all goes

Nigel folds his hands over his eyes.

doesn't want to talk about the past, at least now. just wants to lay on the floor and read off some wallpaper. you're gonna tell me it's not funny the way things go?

Jess opens her document on the computer. She scrolls to the bottom of the page. Mandy stares at the place where the streetlight lands on the asphalt.

would she do that? would she spend months making me feel like i'm not good enough then criticize me for caring about her?

Jess returns to his page. She hovers over his picture with her mouse.

144

why do you exist? why do you have to be here now,
making everything so much more difficult

She stares at the page.

if nothing else, at least i ruined his night yesterday,
made him stay in his office working, didn't submit his paperwork
until midnight. at least i made him sweat up there

She hears Mandy pouring another glass of water in the
kitchen.

probably only took him so long because he had to pull
stuff out of his ass, his methodologies. at least i put some
pressure on him. he had to walk home in the middle of the night

Jess stares at the screen for another moment, then she
begins to rub her eyes.

i've never been on campus that late. too creepy, walking
home late at night. just like Nigel must have been walking home,
leaving the library

Jess looks up at the ceiling. Suddenly her eyes grow
wide.

wait. just wait.

"Mandy, can you come in here?" Jess calls into the
kitchen. Mandy emerges a moment later.

"What is it? What's wrong?"

"Do you remember when Randell said he was expecting
Nigel to get home? Do you remember?"

"I think he said he was expecting him in the evening.
But evening for Nigel I guess means something different than it
means for us."

"Okay, I have to tell you this. I was at Anderson's office
this morning. She was checking to see if Whiteside had
submitted his paperwork for the review. The system said that he
didn't submit his files until midnight."

"What does that mean?"

"That means he was on campus at midnight, leaving
Anthony hall where his office is."

145

"And you think…"

"Yeah! Well just think about it. They could have crossed paths. Anthony hall is right there by the library. I mean, we think Nigel was attacked, right? That cut on his face, the possible concussion, someone attacked him. Don't you think it's possible that it was him?"

"I mean, I guess it's possible. But he's… I don't know. He has problematic ideas about civil rights, that's true. But does that mean he just attacked somebody? A student?"

"Just think about it, the buildings are right there."

"And you know him. He's spineless. He's…again, it's possible, but how can we know?"

"Well, we could show Nigel a picture of him. He said he remembered the person's face?"

"I don't know. Just shove a picture in his face?"

"We would ask and make sure he's ready for it, of course, not just shove it in his face."

"You really think Whiteside attacked him?"

"I don't know for sure. But there's a chance and it's worth reaching out to Nigel about it."

"Well, should we call them?"

"I didn't get Randell's phone number, did you?"

"No, and Nigel doesn't have a phone."

"Right. Well, what about Lapis? She stayed with them."

"I doubt she's still there, but we could try."

"Okay, you call her, I'll get ready."

"Wait, you want to go back over there tonight? What time is it? Jess, it's almost five in the morning already."

"The meeting's at eight. If we don't figure this out now, there won't be time in a few hours. No sleep."

"Why before the meeting?"

"Because I'm gonna expose that motherfucker at the meeting, that's why!"

"Wow. Okay, that'll certainly send a message. If you're right about this."

"Call Lapis and see if she's still over there."

Jess walks to the bathroom. She turns on the faucet and splashes some water on her face. She walks back to the living room and sees Mandy holding the phone to her ear.

"Hey Lapis, sorry to bother you. We're just wondering if you're still with Randell and Nigel... you are, that's good... Well we have some information; a theory I guess you could say. We think we know who attacked Nigel and we want to show him a picture and see if he can confirm it. If he's comfortable with that, of course."

Lapis lowers the phone.

"Mandy says that they think they might know the person you met last night. They're wondering if they can come over and show it to you."

"Can't they just send it to you? It's not 1998," Randell says.

"Is it possible to send it to me and I can show him?" Lapis asks. She glances again at Nigel. "I think he's a little worn out."

"I guess that's probably a better option," Mandy replies. "Jess, they're wondering if we can just send it over. Because it's so late and he's tired."

Jess stops in the middle of the room.

"Yeah. Sure, that works."

"Okay, we'll send it over right now."

"Thank you so much, I'll talk to you soon."

Lapis sets the phone face-up on the floor next to her.

"Well, that will be interesting...to see what their idea is," Randell says.

"Nigel," Lapis begins. "Are you sure you're comfortable with that?"

"Yes, I'm comfortable with that."

147

"I want to ask you about what's going on in the scroll. Where are you getting this stuff? I've never seen anything like it before."

"I don't know where it came from. Maybe from the problem itself."

"Did she send you the picture yet?" Randell asks.

"I don't see it yet," she says quickly before turning back to Nigel.

"I'd love to ask you more about it some other time when things are less chaotic and stressful. That line, where was it…"

She sees her phone light up again. She picks it up and opens the message.

"Okay, I have the picture here. Are you ready to check it out?"

"Yes, I'm ready."

Lapis holds the phone out towards Nigel. She watches his face turn cold.

"Is that him man? Do you recognize him?" Randell asks, rising from his position.

Nigel looks at the image for several seconds, his face expressionless.

"Is he the guy?" Randell asks again.

"Let him process it," Lapis whispers.

After a long silence, Nigel looks away from the picture. Lapis sets the phone on the floor.

"I told you I don't know where he came from," he says softly. "Maybe from sometime long ago, or maybe somewhere closer, much closer."

"Do you recognize him?" Lapis asks gently.

"A fragile anger running underneath everything, a weakness that hurts people." Nigel's voice begins to tremble.

"Hey, you're alright, Nigel. It's okay."

"And this screaming need to control everything, this weakness...needing to keep everything tightly together."

148

His body begins to shake as he speaks.

"You're safe, Nigel. It's okay."

"I know it is," he says through trembling lips. "It's okay because of the music. Because it arrives and escapes and you don't know where you are."

They sit in silence for a moment. Randell begins to pace the floor slowly. Lapis watches Nigel lean back against the wall.

"Was that who did it?" she asks softly.

that screaming need to be in control, that terrible fear

"Yes. It was him. I don't want to know his name."

Randell walks across the room and takes a seat next to Nigel, leaning against the wall.

"That's a brave thing to look at his face again. You know that right? You're a big brave soul."

He sets his hand on Nigel's shoulder and squeezes it gently.

"A brave guy, that's what you are. Just need to rest now. But no goin to sleep just in case it's a concussion."

"I'll let them know," Lapis says, bringing the phone to her ear.

"We'll just stay up. No problem for you right? You never go to sleep."

"Right now, I wish I could."

"I hear you, man. I know. We'll stay up and talk, that's what we'll do. I'll be like your janitor friend at the library. Wonder how he's doing tonight."

"He probably wonders where I am."

"You'll be back soon. Get your nog healed up and you'll be right back there dreamin up new things for people to think about."

"She didn't answer," Lapis says. "Maybe they fell asleep."

"No way. They wouldn't fall asleep now. Look out the window."

149

"Oh. I didn't realize...but...how? Already?"

"Sun doesn't wait," he says. "See that, Nigel? Sun's rising over there, just over the top of the mountains over there."

"I'll go over there and check in with them."

"They're asleep. Why not just go back to your place, or stay here if you want? Sleep on the couch for a few hours, then we'll start back at this in a few hours."

"No, I can't do that. I think I might have an idea of what they're thinking. I'm going over there."

"Well, we'll be up. Call in when you get the chance, caller number five wins a free weekend down at..."

"Make sure he's okay. I'll call you when I find out more."

She closes the door behind her. Randell hears the sound of her boots thumping down the stairs and feels the building rattle when she closes the outer door."

"Well, alrighty then. How should we spend our Friday morning? Probably not too late to get out on the lake and look at the birds."

Nigel sits silently, staring at the wallpaper.

"You sure did a good job with that thing. Never ever would I have thought you were writing on that thing the whole time. Lapis seemed to like what you wrote. I know I couldn't get much out of it."

"You've done lots of different kinds of jobs in your life, haven't you?"

"Well, my fair share I'd say. Why?"

"Have you ever installed wallpaper?"

Mandy reaches down to plug her phone into a charger.

"I'm sure she tried to call back just after it died. When it comes back on, I'll call her again."

Jess sits in front of her computer holding a mug in her hands.

"Maybe I got too excited. I don't know, it just all came together in my mind. The buildings, the time frame. Maybe she didn't call back."

"We'll see, it won't take too long before the phone comes back on."

They hear a knock at the door.

"At six in the morning?"

Mandy opens the door.

"Hey! It's you, my phone died, we were wondering if you'd called back or not. Come in."

Lapis steps through the doorway and into the living room.

"Sorry for bursting in like this, but I decided I needed to come over."

"Did he recognize him?"

"He said it was him, that's the guy."

Jess falls back into the couch for a moment then rises to her feet.

"You're not kidding. He recognized him and said that's the person."

"He was really shaken up when we saw the photo. It took him a little bit to get it out, but he said it was him."

"That's our instructor," Mandy says.

"That's what I was wondering. Wow, how did you know it was him?"

"I didn't," Jess says, "but I knew he was on campus, in the adjacent building, at the same time. They would have crossed paths. And I know that he's an asshole, so there's that too."

"And he's the one who's going under review this morning?"

"He's the one. In 90 minutes."

"Are you going? You said you couldn't go right?"

"Of course, I'm going. And I'm gonna tell them what he did."

151

Jess walks to the kitchen. Mandy and Lapis hear the sound of water against metal.

"Are you going too?" Lapis asks.

"No," Jess calls from the kitchen. "Nobody else."

"But why?"

Lapis follows Jess to the kitchen, Mandy trailing behind her.

"Maybe we should both come with you. We could validate your claim."

"I know how they operate. I know how they make decisions. Anderson and the others will be intimidated by me showing up alone. Bringing a group, they'll think I'm trying to start a fight."

"Listen to yourself," Mandy says. "What are you saying? That you don't want to intimidate them? Of course, you do, and that's the right move. Why do you suddenly want to appeal to their sense of order and decorum? Why?"

"She's right," Lapis says. "There's no sense in playing by their rules now, not when we have all the leverage."

Jess sets the tea kettle on the counter.

"They need a wake-up call. They're long overdue," Mandy says.

"Okay," Jess says after a pause. "You're right. It's just... I don't know."

She sets the kettle on the stove top.

"I'm just tired, I guess. A little caffeine will help. I'll drink this tea then I'll be charged up and ready to go again."

"It's okay to be tired, it makes perfect sense. We didn't sleep at all. We've been awake for like 36 hours straight. But that's all the more reason we should come with you."

"Why?"

"Because you don't have to do it alone. You've already spent so much emotional energy on this, being tired is totally understandable. But if we lean into it together, spread that energy out a little, I think we'll make some noise in there."

Jess glances up from the floor.

what's into her? what's this new voice? and from where and she's really so gorgeous

"Your kettle's almost boiling," Mandy says. "What are you having, green?"

when we would walk to the car in parking lot and kiss under the streetlights

"Jess. Green?"

"Yeah," she says. "Green works. Just a little caffeine. Lapis?"

"Yeah?"

"Before we go any further, can you call them again and ask if Nigel is okay with us telling his story to them? That's a really important part of this. And I feel bad for not thinking of it sooner."

"Yeah, of course, I'll call Randell right now."

"Hopefully they're still awake."

"They are, they're awake," Lapis says bringing the phone to her ear and stepping into the living room.

Randell wrestles the phone from his pocket. He hands the spray bottle to Nigel.

"Lapis again. Let's see what she's up to over there."

Nigel sets the spray bottle on the counter above them and turns to lean back against a cupboard.

"Hey, how's it going...yeah we're doing pretty well over here, got a little project going.... yeah.... yeah, he's here.... sure, here he is."

Randell hands the phone to Nigel.

"Hey, Lapis...yes, I'm feeling better."

"That's good to hear. I have a question for you."

She takes a seat on the couch and switches the phone to her other ear.

"We know the person you met on Wednesday night. I know you said you don't want to know who he is. Coincidently, though, Jess knows him. She actually has a meeting with him this morning. It's a meeting with some of his coworkers. We were wondering if you want us to let those people know about what he did. Is that something you want us to do?"

Nigel's silent for a moment.

"What's she asking? Put it on speaker."

"Does that sound like what you want to do?"

Nigel doesn't say anything.

dreaming in the dancing shadows walking down the street

"Put it on speaker I want to hear her."

"We just want to help bring justice."

"What's she saying?"

entangled with everywhere

"I… I don't want to be…"

"What was her question?"

"You don't want to be what Nigel?"

"It's just too... Maybe later. Maybe later."

entangled with everyone that's what they told me

"That's not what you want to happen right now, but maybe later?

"Right now…"

He closes his eyes.

the music fled and that's what was left

He opens his eyes again.

"What is she asking Nigel?"

"That's not what I want right now. Maybe later. But for now that's not what I want. Thank you for asking."

"Of course, of course, I'll check in with you guys later, okay?"

"Okay."

154

"Let me see the phone…. she hung up already. What was she asking about?"

"They know who I met Wednesday night. They wanted to know if they could ask him about it at a meeting in front of his coworkers."

"And you're not quite ready for that?"

"Maybe later, but not right now."

"That's fine, big man, that's just fine."

They're silent for a moment. Randell watches the light streaming in through the window above him.

"It's gonna look real good in the mornings with this light on it," he says.

Nigel looks at him for a moment, then up at the window. He begins to smile.

"Yeah. I think it will."

"Well it's not gonna jump on the wall by itself now is it? Hand me that bottle."

"It might," Nigel says, grabbing the spray bottle from the counter above him.

Lapis walks back to the kitchen. She sees Mandy spreading peanut butter onto a piece of toast. Jess holds her mug in both hands. They're silent.

"You heard that from in here?"

"Most of it. He said no?"

"Yeah, he said no."

"Well, I can understand that. He's not ready to come forward with his story. I feel bad we were so quick to jump on it."

"It was a lot really fast. We caught ourselves before we got too far," Jess says. She lifts the mug to her lips.

"What do you want to do now?" Lapis asks.

"Leave in five minutes?"

"For the meeting?"

155

"Is that enough time? I just need to pour this into a cup and I'm ready."

"But we can't tell them about what happened."

"Of course not. If Nigel wants to share that story later, that's his choice. It's his story to tell. But we still have a story to tell. Are you both still in?"

Lapis turns to Mandy.

"I have to get a jacket. Then I'm ready. Do you need anything Lapis?"

"Maybe a bite of the toast."

"Go ahead. I'll be right back."

Lapis takes a bite of the toast as she looks out the window.

"It's a bright morning," she says.

"A great morning to fuck that guy's shit up," Jess says, pouring the tea into a cup.

"You know what I just realized?" Randell says as he stands up and straightens out his back.

"What's that?"

"I had work at the store last night. Didn't even think about it. Didn't call in. No show no call's a good way to get fired."

"I'm sorry I disappeared."

"Don't sweat it man. It was a bad job. Plenty of other places to work, warehouse over there a few blocks away. I'll find a new job. It's no sweat."

"But I'm sorry I ran away."

"Hey, you don't have to beat yourself up. Shit happens, I get it. But we figured it out."

He watches Nigel continue to line up the pieces of wallpaper.

ran away. ran up in the woods

He lines the pieces up carefully.

156

maybe that's what she thinks about me. he ran away. he ran off into the city, ran downtown, where he found me

"You know, there's something I've wondered about all this time."

"What's that?"

"Why me? I mean I was just sitting there on that bench. I didn't even notice you coming until you were right there in front of me."

"Why you?"

"Yeah, why me? You didn't know me. You didn't know what I'd done, my past. But you said hell with it I'm gonna be this guy's friend."

Nigel looks up from the wallpaper.

"You're wondering why I asked if you wanted to live here?"

"Yeah, exactly."

"You needed a place to stay. And that room was empty."

He brings his eyes back to the wallpaper. Randell leans back against the cupboard. He smiles to himself.

that's just him i guess. can't always explain a thing like that.

They work in silence for another few moments before Randell stands up again.

"Lapis might be disappointed she doesn't get to finish reading what you wrote on this thing. You had her hanging on every word. I could have used some pointers from you back in the old days."

"Do you want to be together with her again?"

"No way. That's over for us. Too much stuff attached to that. Could never get back to how it was like before. It's sad, but it's true. But we had our time. And I gotta say it's nice having her around. Maybe she'll come hang out with us again, if you're there."

"You're entangled."

157

"What was that?"

"Entangled. And that's what makes you free."

"And that's what makes me free. I'll have to sit on that for a while. Now where'd you say the adhesive was?"

"It's on the top floor," Jess says as she pulls open the large wooden door of Anthony hall.

"The conference room on the top floor."

They cross the polished wooden floor of the foyer quickly, cutting through the columns of dusty light cast on the floor from the big windows.

"What time is it?" Lapis asks.

"Five minutes to eight. Almost go-time."

They reach the staircase at the other end of the foyer and enter the narrow stairwell.

"We'll make a big entrance. Just when they're about to get going, we crash the party."

Their boots ring in the stairwell.

"When we get to the door, I'll start. Jump in when you feel like you need to."

They reach the top floor and turn into the hallway. They hear voices coming from down the hall.

"They're in there. Here we go."

Jess takes long, deliberate strides. She strikes her heels against the tile floors.

here we go, let it happen

She pauses for an instant when they reach the door. They hear muffled voices from inside. She turns and nods at Mandy, then at Lapis, before she pulls open the door.

A small group sits around the large conference table. Whiteside looks up from a stack of papers in front of him. He sits on the right side of the room next to another instructor, facing the door. Professor Anderson sits on the opposite side of the table, along with several other faculty members.

"Glad you didn't start without us," Jess says.

Anderson turns around when she hears Jess' voice.

"Jess, what are you doing here? I told you this meeting is for faculty only."

"Well, we decided that if you're not going to offer us a seat at the table, then we'll just have to take it ourselves."

Heads turn around the room as the group as the group circles the table. They take seats in the far corner of the room, facing both Anderson and Whiteside.

"We spoke about this yesterday, Jess, and I thought we arrived at a clear understanding. This meeting is designed for our faculty to convene and discuss an internal affair. I would be happy to meet with you later to discuss your concerns, but your presence here is disruptive."

"Ah, disruptive. Nice one, that's what resisting authority is now."

Mandy watches Whiteside fidget in his seat, shuffling his papers, taking a drink from his water bottle. She watches his hands shake as he lifts the bottle to his mouth and notices the faint purple bruise running down his finger.

a bruise, right on his finger, in the middle of all this, unbelievable

"I just want to know if anyone else thinks that we're being disruptive. Maybe some of your colleagues would appreciate our input in this matter. Maybe they think that our opinion is relevant to this review."

"Lance," Jess says to the man sitting beside Anderson, "we know each other, I've taken your class. We have legitimate concerns about the process that's going on today. Do you think we're being disruptive? Or Professor Said, do you think it's so crazy for us to get to have some input here? This meeting is the

159

result of my complaint. I'm the reason you're all here at 8 A.M. on a Friday. Let's just cut through it."

Jess pauses and looks out at the faculty sitting across the room. They stare back silently, their faces fixed and emotionless, hovering above the table. Lapis scans the room slowly.

is this what they do? they sit in these rooms up here and have these meetings

Jess meets Whiteside's eyes. He glances away quickly, continuing to shuffle his papers.

that's him, that's the man who did it

Anderson sighs and closes her computer.

"Well, I was about to read the complaint we had worked on together. But because you're here, I suppose you could convey your concerns to everyone here."

"It's really simple. I believe Mark Whiteside has serious flaws in both his teaching methodology and in his ideological framework. I don't intend any unwarranted disrespect, but he's unqualified to teach in this department. I've been particularly disturbed over the past few weeks by his white-washed portrayal of history."

"What do you mean by a white-washed portrayal of history?" Professor Said asks.

"I mean a version of history which erases the critical struggles marginalized groups have always faced in their pursuit of basic human rights. A version of history which counts whatever victories have been won as products of white male legislators giving people freedom with a magic wand."

"I think you're being a little... reductive in that synopsis," Whiteside says.

Jess turns from Professor Said to face him.

so he decided to show up

"What's reductive about it? I'm telling them my experience. I have plenty of documents to back it up. Lecture slides, when there are slides, notes. Even the assignments are

160

about steering students towards that version of history. I'm sure Professor Anderson has shared with you all those documents…"

"But you've failed to mention the breadth of topics and history that I'm covering in that class. It's meant to survey history through the lens of political violence. I've been instructed, by people in this room and others, to offer a wide look at history and the way politically motivated violence has acted on it."

Mandy shakes her head slowly as he speaks. She picks up immediately when he's finished.

"And so, in the process of offering a broad view of history you've decided that people of color, the LGBTQ community, that marginalized groups are merely the recipients of freedom in a slow, but steady march towards equality. Once governments decide that they finally deserve their human rights of course."

"See, I told you," Whiteside says, gesturing towards Anderson, "these are the kinds of gross simplifications I was telling you about."

and they're just bitching at me, just bitch bitch bitch equality and leftwing garbage

"Again, like Jess said, the documentation is there. You can draw your own conclusions about what the instructional goal of these assignments are, but we're not going to let you say that we're being simplistic or reductive when we're arguing for the exact opposite. We want more complexity in our conversations, not less. We think it's possible to analyze a wide swathe of history but still acknowledge the violence that pervades every aspect of this country's history. It's not only possible, it's necessary. And if you can't see that, then something's seriously wrong."

The faces in the room turn back towards Whiteside, expecting a response. He sees their glances.

161

all that critical theory bullshit, the same thing regurgitated over and over

"Be my guest. Look at the documents. This is an accredited course and I'm drawing upon all the materials I was advised to draw upon when I was assigned this course."

twisting their little stories about violence and pain, that's all we're supposed to do is twist little stories

"I, for one, I'm glad they were allowed to speak. That's the strength of a university, its ability to produce ideas from different points of view, the marketplace of ideas as it's sometimes called."

like they really care about ideas, just twisting little stories

Lapis watches Whiteside as he speaks, watching the movements of his eyes and hands.

something so painful inside him the brokenness that Nigel saw, the fracture, you can see it, the pain but it's deeper and twisted tightly.

"But I'm sure everyone has other plans for the day, and we all know how this building heats up as the sun gets higher…"

it's not even pain anymore

"So if we could proceed, I think that would be best for all parties."

it's hate…hate so deep he doesn't know what to do with it

"You can't shut us up," Jess says. "You won't get rid of us. If nothing happens today, we'll be back next week. And again and again until something changes."

it's what Nigel wrote on the scroll, what was it, the entangled…

Mandy stares at Whiteside, she feels anger rising inside her.

how could you do it how could you do something like that

162

"Justice is coming. You won't see it coming, and you'll fight it when it arrives. And you'll lose," she says.

"I think we've said what we wanted to say. Anything to add, Lapis?"

"Justice will win," she says, looking out at the table of faces. "Truth will win. You can't stop it."

They rise from their chairs and walk to the door. Jess holds it open to allow Lapis and Mandy to exit the room. As she turns to leave, she meets Whiteside's eyes again, holding him there in front of her.

same story, same twisted story
the truth wins, you can't stop it

"See you on Tuesday," she says as she closes the door behind her.

The dew still rests lightly on the grass when they push open the wooden front doors and walk slowly down the stone stairs. They pass under the shade of the building as they join the walkway on 10th Street.

"Well, we did something," Lapis says as they walk. "You two were really great in there."

"It's not over," Jess says. "It's far from over. If they didn't hear us today, they'll hear from us again."

The soft yellow light falls gently through the trees lining the walkway.

"I think it's time for a nap," Mandy says. "It's been a long... I don't even know. Day, night, week. And Lapis, you have your show tonight, I almost forgot."

"You and me both. Do you two want to come?"

"I'm not missing it," Jess says. "Invite Randell and Nigel too if they're up for it."

They pass under the row of scarlet oaks, lit up bright red by the rising sun.

"This is where I turn," Lapis says. "But I hope I see you there tonight!"

163

"You will," Mandy says. "Thank you again for going in there with us."

They stand under the scarlet oaks, pausing in the glow of the sunlight.

"You two go take your nap, I'll see you tonight," Lapis says.

As they walk opposite ways down the sidewalk, Lapis places her hands in the pockets of her flannel, watching the distant clouds glide slowly over the mountains in the distance.

"A nap will be good," Jess says.

"Yeah. Yeah, it will be good."

Jess holds out her hand for Mandy, who takes it warmly.

The scarlet oaks shimmer in the morning light. The red leaves fall softly before them on the sidewalk.

"What's the verdict? Does it do what it's supposed to do?"

Randell watches Nigel closely. He steps forward and touches the wall, running his fingers over it. He closes his eyes.

"Whatya think? Good? Bad? Could always run down to the store and get some more. That would sure be one way to spend a Friday night."

Nigel spreads his hands out over the wallpaper, sliding them back and forth.

"We could go into business with this stuff. That is if being a poetry philosopher guy doesn't work out for you."

Nigel feels it rising in his chest. He watches it, allows it to grow.

arriving and departing, concealment and ecstasy, watching

"You know they make paper for writing too. You don't only have to write on wallpaper."

and being watched. looking and begin looked at

Nigel opens his eyes. Randell leans against the counter. He feels the cool afternoon air on his neck from the open window.

"Yeah, this will work for now."

"Well, holy shit, that's what I like to hear! It works for now. Well, just let me know next time, we'll stick a new one up there."

"Randell," Nigel says.

"What is it bud?" Randell says pushing himself up to a seated position on the counter.

"Thank you for being my friend."

"Hey, of course big man you're my guy."

Nigel walks into the living room and takes a book from his shelf. Randell sits on the counter, looking at the wall.

of course. of course. i'll always be there for you big man

He feels a buzz in his pocket.

there's the lady from the store telling me not to come in tonight i bet

He wrestles the phone from his pocket.

oh, it's Lapis...has a show tonight. guess i'll ask him

"Hey Nigel," he calls from the kitchen, "Lapis wants to know if we can come to her show tonight, you in?"

Nigel doesn't respond.

"I'm sure she'd appreciate you being there," he says.

"Okay," Nigel says. "But let me get some reading done first."

"You betcha. Leave here in a couple hours."

Randell hops off the counter. He turns to look out the window, watching the trees sway in the breeze. In the distance, he sees a group of clouds stacked over the mountains.

maybe. it may be

there she is
"She's up next, come on, let's get to the front. Excuse me, don't sweat on me please."
she's up next
"I told you, lots of sweaty men at things like this."
there she is and she looks great
"Come on, let's get all the way to the front."
Lapis sits on the stool on the elevated platform.
hey, she's up there we made it
"Outta the way. Hey watch out. Okay, that guy's blacked out."
she's already up there and she's nervous you can tell
"Let's try to get to the front I see Jess and Mandy up there."
entangled, deeply entangled
"Hey! You guys made it. Good to see you Nigel!"
"Okay, she's starting."
Lapis begins strumming the guitar. The crowd quiets down as they hear her opening chords.
she's good, she can really play
she still can play, even though she looks so nervous. but wait till they hear her sing
Lapis leans forward and begins to sing softly.
wow that's her voice that's what her voice sounds like no fucking way
she's a good singer
sang like that in the trees, at the lake, sure is good to hear that voice
Her voice floats over the crowd and out the door.
you would never know she could sing like that if you didn't know her, that's the way it is i guess
that's a voice like nothing i've ever heard. like nothing is ever wrong, like nothing will ever hurt, just go and live and be everything you can. but her voice will always be in your ear,

166

*right there just out of reach. and you feel like you do when you
know something is ending that will never happen again. you wish
you could have it there for just a little longer. but it's receding
away*

*and you know when you hear her that you'll never hear
nothing like it again, and it makes you sad. but it's like when
something's ending and you didn't even know it was happening.
you just sit back and remember what it was like. and that's
almost enough*

entangled

Lapis steps off the platform and brings the guitar to her
side as the crowd cheers loudly.

"That was great! Amazing! You were amazing!"

"Why didn't you tell us you could sing like that? You're
incredible."

"Thank you, I was nervous. I haven't played in front of
people in so long. Nigel and Randell, came! I'm so happy you
came! Here, can we step outside for a little and get some air?"

They push through the crowd slowly, out the door, and
into the cool night.

"That's better. Thank you guys so much for coming, it
made me feel a lot better seeing you all there in the front. I
pretended like I was just playing for you."

"You did so good. You're amazing."

"I did okay. It felt good being up there. I want to do it
again."

"You should. And soon. And invite all of us again."

"Totally. It's kind of funny. Some of us have only
known each other for a couple of days, but it feels like so much
longer."

"Hiking up a mountain in the middle of the night will do
that to you I guess," Nigel says.

167

"You're the only person I can think of right now I would hike up a mountain at night for," Jess says.

"Here, let's all take a picture. Is that okay? Let's take a picture."

Lapis hands her phone to a person nearby. They huddle together for the picture.

"Thank you so much," she says, taking the phone back from the person. "I don't know if these look good or not but I just wanted to have this night saved, for memory's sake. What are you all doing now?"

"I think going home is our next move," Mandy says. "Maybe we should do something else this weekend. Go to the park or something if it's nice."

"Absolutely, let me know! Have a great night you two!"

"Are you two okay to walk home?" Randell asks.

"Yeah, we're okay. It's just a block around the corner."

"Okay, be safe, see you!"

"Great job again! You're amazing!" Mandy calls back to Lapis as they walk towards the corner. When they disappear around it, Lapis turns back to Randell and Nigel.

"It means so much that you guys came tonight," she says.

"You did great, really you're a natural up there."

i had almost forgotten

"Can we walk you home?" Nigel asks.

"That would be really great, thank you for asking Nigel."

"Do you live close by?"

"Just a couple blocks west of here."

"Might not be too far from us. We live that way."

that would sure put the varnish on it. if she lived right by us all this time. that would sure do it

The sound from the house grows quieter as they walk under the dark trees.

"Are you feeling any better Nigel?" Lapis asks after a moment.

"Yes, much better. We had a good day."

"Well, that's good! What did you do?"

"We installed the wallpaper."

"You what?"

"We installed the wallpaper."

"The blue one, with the birds on it?"

"Yes, we did."

"But Nigel, you wrote something amazing on that. And you hung it up in your apartment."

"Yes, we did."

"Is that what you wanted to do?"

"Of course."

"I really liked what you wrote on the back of it."

As they pass the row of scarlet oaks on the edge of the university campus, Nigel stops suddenly on the sidewalk.

"What's up? Are you okay?"

He turns to look through the row of trees, down the dark street, towards the glow of the lights illuminating the front face of the library.

"I want to go in there for a while."

"Come on, man, it's been a long day. Let's just go home.

"I really need to be in there for a while."

"But isn't it closed at this hour on a Friday?"

"Jason will let me in."

"How long do you want to stay?"

"For a while. I just need to be there."

"Okay, how about I come back and meet you in front in two hours? Is that enough time?"

"Yes. That's enough time."

"Alright, enjoy yourself in there. I'll see you back out here in two hours."

169

"Have a good time, Nigel!" Lapis calls as he passes under the row of trees. "Thanks again for coming to the show!"

They stand and wait until the brass door of the building opens from within and Nigel steps inside before carrying on down the street.

"He loves being in there. That's his favorite place to be. I knew he would want to be back as soon as he could."

"Why do you want to walk him home?"

"I would just feel better about it. After what happened couple nights ago."

"You're a great friend for him."

"I don't know. I could be better. I've gotten frustrated with him before."

"That happens between friends."

"Yeah."

"So you put up that wallpaper? You really did?"

"We did. I knew you wouldn't be too happy about it. But right after you left this morning he just insisted. He had the stuff in his room. We had a good time with it."

"Some of the things he wrote on that thing...I wasn't sure where I was reading it. But then some of the things were clear as day, but still made you think. What was that one thing he wrote? I need to think about it."

They cross another street. Randell glances up at the clouds.

maybe. it may be time

"Here's the alley up here," he says.

"Mine is another street down. I guess we do live pretty close. I was kind of disoriented this morning when they dropped us off."

"Do you like living here? In the city?"

"Absolutely. There's so much life and opportunity. Like tonight. You couldn't have something like that back home."

"No. I guess you couldn't."

"But you're asking if I ever miss being out there?"

"No. Of course not. Who would miss living out there?"

"Sometimes. When I'm falling asleep, just before I drift off, I pretend I'm back at the orchard, underneath the trees, all that sweetness just swallowing me. Do you ever think of things like that?"

"The lake. Being out there by the lake. Especially in the mornings. And at night. And I think about that orchard too. And the flies."

that smile in the moonlight under those trees and her eyes

"I do want to go back someday. I told the family back there that I would. Maybe this summer. Go back and work."

"You should. They love you there. It's not a bad place over there. I know things happened with me there, but it's not a bad place. And they gave me a lot."

"But you don't want to go back."

"Not right now. But maybe someday. Go back there and visit. Who knows?"

"I have a question."

"What is it?"

"I want to see what the wallpaper looks like hanging up in your place. Can you show me?"

"Sure. Of course. Not like I'm going to bed for the next two hours. Come on in."

Jess sets her keys on the table and falls onto the couch. Mandy walks to the kitchen and fills a glass of water. Jess presses her face into the cushion, breathing deeply. When she hears Mandy return from the kitchen, she sits up.

"Mandy?"

"Yeah?"

"Can we talk for a little?"

"Yeah. What is it?" she asks, taking a seat next to Jess on the couch.

"I just...want to say I'm really sorry about how I acted last night when I first came in. And the things I said. It wasn't okay. And I know that wasn't the only thing I've done recently to make you feel...like you're not doing enough. I'm just really sorry. I know it wasn't okay."

Mandy hears the shaking in Jess' voice and sees the tears welling up in her eyes. They're silent for a moment.

"You're being vulnerable with me, so I feel like I need to be vulnerable... and honest with you. Things have been bad lately. And that's just as much my fault as it is yours and.... things got bad after everything happened a few months ago. I just...I did start having feelings for Lapis when we first started hanging out. There were a couple days there when I felt like I had feelings for her. I'm so sorry."

She feels hot tears running down her cheeks. Jess holds her head in her hands and sobs quietly.

"I'm sorry," Mandy whispers.

"I knew. That was the thing. I could tell, but so much was happening. But you don't now do you? You don't anymore?"

"No, not anymore."

They cry quietly together without speaking.

"And I'm sorry that I didn't support you in everything you were doing." Mandy says through her tears.

"You tried, you were doing your best, I just wasn't letting you. And today you were so great. You were so great."

"I love you, Jess. I love you more than I ever have before. You're woven into everything that I am, and I want to love you until I fall apart."

"You're the greatest thing that's ever happened to me. And I'll never ever quit loving you."

They wrap up into each other, squeezing tightly, as their tears fall softly on each other's shoulders.

Randell opens the door and switches on a light.

"Here it is," he says. "You can thank Nigel for the inconsistencies in the pattern. He said something about it. I honestly can't remember."

Lapis walks into the kitchen and holds her hand up to the wallpaper.

"It's beautiful," she says quietly.

"It does sorta look like it belongs in someone's grandma's house. But it has a nice look to it. And he'll probably want to throw something else on it again before too long."

Nigel sits at his table on the highest floor of the library, hidden behind a stack of books. He scribbles quickly on a piece of paper.

"I have an idea. You might think it's weird, but I don't care," Lapis says.

"What is it?"

"There's a streetlight out the window. If we turn the lights off, we can probably still see the wallpaper."

"You want to turn off the lights and look at the wallpaper."

"Just for a little. Just to see how it looks."

"Hey, your wish is my command," he says, stepping across the room and flipping the switch off.

"Now come back in here," she says.

"Okay."

"Let's look at it."

The streetlamp outside casts a faint light on the center of the wallpaper. Then another light emerges in the corner and begins traveling up across the wall, exiting onto the ceiling.

"I... I don't know what to say."

173

the shadows dancing in the trees

"I remember what Nigel wrote. The part that really stuck out to me"

He scribbles furiously on his piece of paper, filling the page line by line. He pauses for an instant to open a book beside him.

"What was it?" Randell whispers.

Mandy and Jess cuddle into each other, touching their foreheads together, Mandy's finger running down Jess' shoulder.

"I think I can get it word for word."

Nigel steps away from his table, walking across the room to the large windows facing the dark lawns and towers of the university outside.

"What was it?" he whispers again, watching a light run across the wallpaper.

"I'm entangled with everyone I've ever met, even when I'm not with them. Lights meshing together between the shadows, vanishing like fleeting music, appearing like sudden rain."

"Can you hear that?" he asks.

Nigel watches the rain fall from the window in the library.

"Hear what?"

Mandy and Jess listen to the drops of rain falling on the roof as they drift off to sleep.

"It's raining," he says.

They stand before the blue wallpaper in silence, watching the shadows dance, as the sky scatters itself widely from above.

Made in the USA
Coppell, TX
03 July 2020

30056696R00100